# DIRTY PLAYER

A Hockey Romance

## MIRA LYN KELLY

DIRTY PLAYER written and published by Mira Lyn Kelly

© 2018 by Mira Lyn Kelly

Cover design by Mira Lyn Kelly

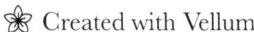 Created with Vellum

## About The Book

**He'll play dirty to get his girl**

**It started as a joke…**

A throw away promise between friends.

A dare for a single kiss at our reunion and nothing more.

**But that kiss…**

That kiss was no joking matter.

It was hot and wet.

A hands-everywhere, breathless kind of insanity that left us both teetering on the brink.

**She's got rules about dating guys like me…**

Rules I respect the hell out of when they apply to any other pro athlete.

But as they apply to me? Well, those rules are about to be broken.

*For Zoe York*

# Newsletter

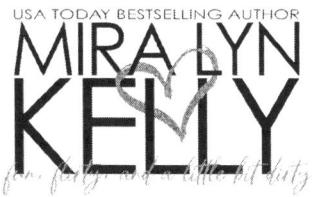

Want to stay in the know about all of Mira's new releases, giveaways and fun??
Sign up for her newsletter at
miralynkelly.com/newsletter

## Chapter 1

*Greg*

"*N*O GAG REFLEX, you don't say?"

This is what I get for coming to the rookie's housewarming party. Preseason's barely started and already I've lost interest in the puck bunnies. Cracking the cap on the water I pulled out of the built-in fridge, I take a long swallow. Should have stayed home to catch up on the *The Walking Dead*.

The bleach blonde with enhanced everything leans into me, pressing her tits against my arm.

"Uh-huh." She plucks a wad of gum from between her lips, stretching and twisting it around her finger, before blinking up at me with a promise-filled smile. "I could show you."

And in case I'm somehow missing the deeper meaning, she goes for my junk.

Dodging out of reach, I give Grabby Hands a look that assures I'm both surprised and delighted by her incredibly thoughtful offer. It comes with the wink and smile that have been getting me in and out of trouble from as far back as I can remember… and a hard pass. But a *nice* one.

I'm not a dick. I'm just not interested in the bunny my right winger backdoored last week. Sweet as I'm sure she is.

Grabby heads off in search of her next box to check, and my teammate Ruxton Meyers strolls over, eyes glued to her swaying ass.

"What I wouldn't give *not* to know where she's been." He rubs his mouth with a scarred knuckle.

"Or that Vsevolod didn't wear a rubber?" I offer with an evil smirk.

Rux's head snaps around.

"I think my dick just crawled back into my body, dragging the boys along."

I laugh. "Probably the safest place for them."

Vsevolod's a good kid and a fucking great hockey player, but at nineteen he's got even less sense about women and self-preservation than I did at that age. I've tried to warn him, like the older guys tried to warn me. But he'll have to figure it out on his own. I just hope it happens before his dick falls off or some bunny in a three-inch skirt "accidentally" gets knocked up for the sole purpose of hitching herself to his bank account.

"What the hell?" Rux asks, distracted by the roar from the front room. "Baxter, man, he put on football."

*Football?* "*Et tu*, Vsev?"

Only then, I get a better look at the screen, and it's not actually the *game* he's got on, but the sideline interview. Or rather, the *reporter.* He's paused the feed so her face fills the screen.

Like always, I recognize the twenty-four-karat shine of her hair, the full lips that launched a thousand dirty high-school fantasies, and the heavy-lidded eyes that seem to be perpetually gleaming with some kind of private joke. Julia Wesley. The coolest girl at Bearings High, and one of the few with the good sense to shut me down.

That good sense is why, ten years later, we're friendly enough that I'm pulling out my phone to grab a shot of Vsevolod pointing to her lips.

Little pervert.

She's going to love this.

**Me: He swears he doesn't actually watch the games… he just beats it to the interviews.**

It's less than ten seconds before her message pops up.

**Julia: You ass! Is that Vsev? God, now I need a shower.**

I grin. Of course she knows who he is. Football is her bread and butter, but Jules knows her sports and is privy to more locker room gossip than I am. So her disgust at making it into his spank bank is based on information above the average joe's pay grade.

**Me: Absolutely, you should take one. Send me a picture.**

Five seconds this time.

**Julia: In your dreams.**
**Me: More than once.**

It's been a few years, but I'm serious. We might be friends of the *just* variety, but Julia Wesley's a stone-cold fox. Wood-worthy in all the best ways—most of which have less to do with her slamming bod and more to do with her mouth and, specifically, what comes out of it. The girl's sharp as fuck, knows more about sports than anyone I've ever met, and *her confidence*. Damn. I adjust my fly, sending a silent reprimand to the man downstairs. We've been through this before. He knows better.

Regardless, the big guy's got his back up, and I can't blame him.

**Me: Ready for the reunion next week?**

I imagine her shaking head and a huff of breath tossing a bit of blonde from her eyes. Maybe some muttering. She's working a game, so no dirty four-letter words.

Shame.

A full minute passes.

**Julia: The reunion, yes. The rest? You can't seriously think that's going to happen.**

I don't, but no way am I going to tell her that. This is way too much fun. Instead, I fire off the picture I took from my yearbook two weeks ago, my chicken scratch "contract" taking up a page in the back:

> PRESUMING WE ARE BOTH STILL SINGLE, I, JULIA WESLEY, AGREE TO LET GREG BAXTER KISS ME AT OUR TEN-YEAR REUNION.

BENEATH IS her curvy signature underlined with Xs and Os.

**Julia: Yeah, about that... I think I feel a fiancé coming on. And umm... a really painful cold sore. That tingle. Something's definitely going on there.**

Liar. I grin and pull up Amazon to overnight her a tube of Abreva. I love Prime.

**Me: See you next week.**

---

*Julia*

"COME ON, Julia, let me take you out after the game. What do you say?"

I beam up at Mike Rylan, who's giving me the one-dimpled aww-shucks grin that, combined with his killer combination of dark skin and light eyes, has landed him as many advertising contracts as his throwing arm. He's cute and genuinely nice, one of my favorite players to reach out to in the run-up to game night, but… "You know I don't date football players."

Or any players, for that matter.

"You're breaking my heart," Mike says, placing his hand over his chest pads.

Pretty sure there's a line around the stadium of available women to help him out.

My cameraman Eddie starts flashing a countdown of fingers.

*Three, two, one… On air.*

I turn my smile to the camera and the millions of viewers beyond.

"Mike, what was the tone in the locker room coming into today's game?"

Five questions later, Mike jogs back to his team, and Eddie lowers the camera.

"You know how many women would kill for that guy to give them a second glance, and you've shot him down, what, three times this year alone?"

I laugh, but I take my career and my rule not to date anyone in the sports industry zombie-apocalypse seriously. Which makes me think about this weekend and Greg Baxter's threat to collect on the throwaway promise I made ten years ago.

There's no way he thinks I'm actually going to kiss him.

He's joking. He's *always* joking.

He has to be.

And I have a rule.

Don't get me wrong, Greg's seriously hot, with thick dark hair cut long enough to curl a little at the ends, a brawny built-tough body, and long eyelashes framing the brightest, most sparkly blue eyes I've ever seen. Kissing him would be no hardship. But it would be weird.

We're friends. For-real friends. And that's not something I take lightly.

But even if I did, I've seen too many promising careers derailed by relationships with the wrong men. In my field, reputation is everything. It only takes one screw-up. The smallest hint of a rumor, and all credibility is shot. No way is that going to be me. I've worked too long and too hard to allow some guy to mess with my career.

So ix-nay on the issing-kay with Greg.

Even though I'm sure he's not serious. Mostly sure.

## Chapter 2

THERE ARE A handful of reporters staked out behind the metal gates put up by security when I arrive at the reunion. I stop to shake hands, smile for a few pictures, and laugh when they ask if there's anything I wish I could go back to high school and do again.

"Nah, once was enough."

It's a safe answer, but not even close to the truth. There are too many things to count that I wish I hadn't missed, sacrifices I made for a sport that, at the level I was playing at through high school, meant the exclusion of pretty much everything else. Don't get me wrong, I wouldn't change what I have—no way. But if I could go back, knowing I'd still end up where I am today? Yeah, I'd do it in a heartbeat.

Julia's probably the only person I've ever admitted that to. The only one who really understood.

I smile for a few more pictures and then take the steps up to the front doors.

It hasn't been that long since I've been back to Bearings High. I never actually played with their hockey team, but I've got good memories from my years here, so supporting the program made sense, and walking the halls of the sprawling brick mammoth isn't as unfamiliar to me as it is to some. Still, there's always something strange about pushing through the main doors and walking the locker-lined halls as an adult. The rational part of my mind knows I'm not going to round the corner and find Julia laughing by our lockers, and yet it feels like I'm about to have those honey-brown eyes meet mine anyway.

Tonight's different, though. I know I'll see her, but not hanging out at the end of South Hall.

There's gotta be a few hundred phones at the ready when I make it to the gym. And no, not because of me. Don't get me wrong, my ego is definitely a full-size package, but I'm not conceited enough to think all these people are here to see me. At the reunion, I'm just another graduate from the class, just another guy looking forward to catching up with friends I haven't seen since graduation.

Just another guy looking forward to catching up with Julia.

Speaking of, she's standing at the name tag table,

surrounded by what looks like half the varsity football team she managed from our year, and I laugh, wondering if that's as far as she made it before they swarmed her. Can't really blame them—I caught sight of her three-point-five seconds ago and already I feel the pull to get closer. To see her smile. Make her laugh.

Julia isn't trying to tone down her looks the way she does on the field or at the few network parties where our paths have crossed over the years, so she looks more like herself than I've seen in a long time. Her blonde hair is loose and a little wild, falling in wavy layers that break above her shoulders. Her dress is blue with a lacy top that's fitted across her rack and falls in a flirty tease above her knees. Her eyes have a smoky look to them and her mouth—damn, that mouth has always been my weakness. Wide and full, that mouth has been putting dangerous and dirty ideas in my head since I moved to Bearings my sophomore year to be within range of a Tier 1 team. And tonight, that mouth is glossed pink and spread into the smile I've missed seeing.

I take a step in her direction, but suddenly there are a dozen guys in front of me and someone's pumping my hand like I handed them a check for a million bucks.

"Baxter, man, great game last night!"

"Thanks," I answer back, trying to place faces. One dozen turns to two, and a chorus of voices surrounds me.

I'm used to this after the games and at fan events, but it's different knowing these are the people I went to school with. Worse, because while they all seem to recognize me, I'm only getting hits on about three faces out of the crowd.

---

*Julia*

THE LOOK on Greg Baxter's face is priceless, but what did he expect? He's the local hero, star center for the Chicago Slayers hockey team—who kicked ass last year when they signed him. Greg should have shown up with bodyguards and some razor wire to string around himself.

Things aren't much better over here, but I've been back in Chicago for years. I've been to weddings and baby showers and come home to find my little sister hosting half her old high school class in our apartment. There's less mystery with me. And while we're both nationally recognized, the biggest difference between my crowd tonight and his is that these guys were like family to me in high school. And Greg, well, he didn't have the time to forge those kinds of relationships.

His head comes up and our eyes meet. It's a quick look, followed by the tilt of his lips and a flash of teeth, but it's enough to have me laughing as I turn back to my guys. Enough to make me wonder how far he's going to push the joke sitting between us. Fortunately, it looks like I'll have some time before I have to find out.

"Guys, much as I'd love to hang out all night rehashing games from the glory days, I see a couple people I want to say hi to. Catch up with you in a bit?" The men surrounding me are big, but they've got nothing on the guys I've made my career handling, and I easily cut through the crowd to where a couple of my girlfriends from back in the day are giggling and waving their drinks at me.

Forty-five minutes later, I'm in line for the bar when I feel the skin along the back of my arms and neck begin to heat.

"Hope you brought your cherry ChapStick."

I'd know that low rumbly voice anywhere and, turning around, I offer Greg a cheeky grin. "Why, you got a girl for me to kiss? Think I might like it?"

Greg makes a strangled noise, his eyes glaze over, and his chiseled lips start to curve.

"You're imagining it!" I gasp, swatting at his shoulder and then resisting the temptation to touch it again when I realize how massive it is.

His hands come up between us. "You started it, Jules. Where do you think my mind's going to go when you throw an image of you and Candy like that at me?"

"Candy?"

Greg grins. "I'm a respectful guy. Even scantily clad

ChapStick-lovin' girls conjured by my imagination get names."

I roll my eyes for his benefit, but I should've known better. This is Greg. Over-the-top, outrageous, bad boy Greg Baxter.

Rocking back on his heels, he crosses his arms against his broad chest and looks me over top to bottom. It's not one of those leering, perverted looks— it's one old friend enjoying the sight of another. I know, because I'm doing the same. It's funny, but even though it's been less than a year since I've seen him in person, I'm still struck by how tall he actually is. How he's broader than he looks on TV. And that hair—standing at all angles, it's an artful mess I'm guessing took less than fifteen seconds to perfect. He looks criminally good in his navy suit and tie, but a part of me wishes I could see him back in his worn jeans and one of those well-loved hockey T-shirts that never seemed quite big enough for the body within it.

After a deep breath, he grins and pulls me in for a bear hug that makes this reunion everything I'd hoped it would be.

"It's great to see you."

I close my eyes, enjoying the feel of his big arms around me and the clean, woodsy scent that somehow hasn't changed since high school. "You too, Baxter."

He lets me go and puts a step between us while keeping his rough hand on the back of my arm.

"So when are you gonna stop playing with those football pansies and start covering a real sport?"

I laugh at the old joke between us and nod toward a couple of open seats at a nearby table. I could ask Greg about the game the other night or how his rib has been holding up after the injury from last year. But the answers to those questions are back at my network office, and it's not what I want to know.

"How's it been living back in Chicago—aside from hockey?"

His eyes crinkle at the corners, and he pulls me closer to give me a squeeze.

"The first non-league related question I've gotten all night, and it comes from the sports reporter."

"I had a feeling."

"You always do." He pulls out my chair and we sit, smiling as we look at each other for a moment. Then he answers, "It's good. I like living downtown, and while the bulk of my time is spent with the team, it's nice to be close enough to see Natalie… whenever."

Thinking about Greg's sister puts a smile on my face. He used to call her Goon, like she was a little enforcer on the ice, but when it came to the guys who were interested in her—*he* was the enforcer. "She doesn't play anymore does she?"

"Nah, blew out her knee in college. You know she graduated from Wisconsin, right? But now all her ice time is coaching a 12U girls team. Loves it."

We talk about his parents, who moved back when

he got traded to the Slayers, and me having my sister Cammy and my four-year-old nephew as roommates. About having Jack Hastings as a landlord, and how our former schoolmate thinks the guy who moved into Hank Wagner's old place is a douche. He asks me about my mom, and I'm trying to figure out how to change the subject so I don't have to explain about Florida and what her latest mistake, Chuck, is costing me, when the music cuts off and Tabby Jennison takes the stage at the front of the gym. Greg smirks, and I'm willing to bet dollars to donuts he's thinking of the time she drank too much at Tucker Lawry's party and I had to hold her hair out of the toilet for half an hour before helping him drive her home. It was one of maybe three parties Greg got to attend through all of high school, and he spent it driving a drunk girl home when her own boyfriend wouldn't.

Greg's big hand reaches across the table and pushes my cosmo back, and I know I was right. Like always, I find myself quietly laughing at the unspoken jokes we share, smiling a bit wider because that's what this guy does to me. Always has. I haven't been paying attention to what Tabby's been saying, but suddenly the gym lights go dim, and the spotlights start swirling through the crowd until they land on us and stop.

There's an introduction, and I wave along with Greg, expecting the spot to move on to someone else. Only it doesn't. Tabby's eyes gleam as they meet mine.

"So, about a week ago, I got this text from Julia's

little sister, Cammy, with a picture of an IOU written in the back of Greg Baxter's yearbook."

## Chapter 3

*Greg*

*J*ULIA CHOKES ON her drink, and my spine goes ramrod straight. Shit.

Yeah, I've been working her over about the kiss she owes me, but I know better than to make it public. Privacy is hard enough to come by when our livelihoods are made in the public eye, but hell, I didn't even tell anyone about it ten years ago.

Tabby explains the IOU, looking every kind of delighted as the gym erupts in laughter and cheers around us.

There's only one way to handle something like this. Head-on.

I lean in to Julia, who's pulled it together in a blink and is laughing like the good sport she is. Only I know that inside she's probably freaking the fuck out. She doesn't date athletes or anyone with ties to the networks. She's careful to protect her credibility in ways guys never have to think about. And this, this thing from back when we were kids, isn't something she's going to want taking over the internet.

"Trust me?" I ask, close enough for her to hear over the crowd.

The nod I get back is so small I barely catch it, but it hits me right in the chest.

Trust is a big deal for me.

I stand, signaling the crowd to give me a second. Then, flashing my most troublemaking grin, I take Julia's hand and pull her from her seat.

She's all laughs, but the look in her eyes says she's going to feed me my own balls if I fuck this up.

Not a chance.

I tug her closer, making a show of it, and closer still. Not up against me, though I'm damn certain it would feel amazing. Then I pull this Fred Astaire move on her, quick enough so the only thing she can do is go with it and give up some more of that laughter as I dip her back over my arm.

She's clutching my lapel in a death grip, and those warm honey eyes of hers are wide with shock, but in the next second, she relaxes enough to let me know *she knows* I've got her.

All around us the grown-up versions of the kids we went to school with are laughing and hooting, waiting for me to make my move, and I'm about to when I catch the flicker of Julia's eyes to my mouth and the slight catch of her breath. It's over almost before it starts, but I saw it.

And that look is like lightning through my nervous system, because it wasn't some *please, no, anything but those lips on mine* kind of look. It was, ever so briefly, a hot look. Curious, even.

Fortunately for Julia, I've made my career taking hits that shake me to the core and keeping my senses about me when they happen. So even though my gut and too many other body parts to count have fixated on that single hot second, goading me to take her mouth the way I've always wanted to, I keep my shit together and grin at the crowd.

"Kiss her already," a guy who looks like he might have swallowed the kid who sat beside me in chem cheers.

"Should I?" Turning back to Julia, I look into her eyes and quietly ask for that much more of her trust. "Should I?"

Firmly back in the moment, she huffs a bored breath and gives me what I'm asking for.

"Knock yourself out, stud."

*Stud*. Only Julia.

I dip her back even farther, just to feel the clutch of her hand at my jacket and see the widening of her eyes. Then I pop a puckered-up squeaky kiss on her cheek, close enough to her ear that I've got no doubt the only thing the cameras are catching is her face screwed up into some kind of grimace.

The boos and laughter are in full force as I offer my cheek for the requisite peck in return and then we're done. Both of us are laughing as I pull her back up and put a couple of feet between us.

Her eyes dart to mine, and I can see the relief in them.

No one is going to read anything into this.

I want to talk to her some more, but that ship has sailed. When the crowd pushes between us and twenty different conversations start at once, we go with it.

———

*Julia*

I AM NOT DISAPPOINTED. No way.

That kiss was exactly what I needed it to be—fun, light, nothing that says anything more than Greg and I are old friends. Sure, there was that single crazy second when I got a little drunk looking up into Greg's eyes, but it passed as quickly as it came. And so long as no one knows about it, I've got no worries.

We take the teasing that is our due, laughing with our old classmates, both familiar and not so familiar. Just having a good time.

Greg catches my eye from across the thickening crowd. "Hey, see you later?"

"Absolutely."

After an hour, I've reconnected with several more friends and am still grinning about Missy Evers's shenanigans as I step out of the ladies' room.

"Hey, Jules, hold up."

I startle, finding Greg pushing off the opposite wall where he'd been waiting for me.

I smile. "Thought I might not get another chance to see you tonight."

It's happened before. We've been to corporate events where we haven't been able to clock more than five minutes together the whole night.

He shakes his head, stepping closer. "Didn't think you'd get off that easy, did you?"

"Easy?"

I glance down the locker-lined hall and find it deserted. The music from the gym is muted, and aside from a shriek and giggle echoing from another hall, we're alone.

Our eyes meet, and again that tiny flare of awareness runs through me. But before I can think about it, Greg's caught my hand in his and is firmly pulling me away from the reunion and toward the doors that lead to the track and field complex behind the school.

"Greg!" I half whisper, half laugh, not resisting. I want to see what he's got up his sleeve.

He pushes the exit door open and scans the area. "No one out here. Security blocked off access to the back of the school."

Then he's tugging me out into the cool September night. The sky is a dark purple; the fields and turning trees beyond the spotlit track and parking lot look like black cutouts against the fading light.

"Greg! What are you doing?"

He stops and turns to me, towering close, his eyes in shadow. "You know what I'm doing."

My heart skips a beat. Okay, *now* I do. Only I'm not quite sure how I feel about it. "We kissed. In front of a room full of witnesses." I swallow. "My debt is paid."

"Please," he barks out. "That wasn't even close to a real kiss. And even if it was, that was for them. I want the one you promised *me*." One thick brow arches up. "Come on, Jules. Don't you want to know what it would be like, just once?"

My belly does one of those little roller coaster dips, because this is Greg. My friend.

My incredibly hot and talented friend, who's pressing for the kind of crazy foolishness I'd never even consider outside these all-too-easy-to-write-off circumstances. But if I ever wanted to know, I suppose this is my chance… The free pass I may never have again.

And I mean, I did promise, right?

Smile hitching higher, he nods. "You do want to know! Knew it."

Towing me the rest of the way, he takes a last look around before pulling me under the bleachers.

It's quiet beneath the stands, cool, and darker than in the open, but not so much we can't see. This isn't a place where Greg and I have been before. At least not together. It feels intimate and isolated within the shelter. It feels like I'm back in high school, and all the reasons I usually avoid situations like this don't exist. It feels like for once, I can give in to the moment and just have some fun.

We're standing close. Closer than I ever stand to guys off camera, and I'm hyperaware of the space between us. Of how it shrinks when Greg touches my hair, rubbing it between his fingers and thumb before tucking it behind my ear. He hasn't even touched my skin, but chills skate down my neck and arms, and the air begins to feel thin.

"This is weird," I whisper, looking anywhere but at him.

"You backing out on me?"

"I'm no welcher." I'm aiming to convey how utterly unaffected I am by this whole thing, how *not* seriously I'm taking it—but the crack in my voice betrays me.

Greg smiles. "Nervous?"

I shouldn't be.

This is a joke.

A lark. A dare.

A laugh we'll pass back and forth through the years to come.

So that's what I make it.

I meet Greg's eyes. "Yeah, it's my first time. Be gentle."

Greg scoffs, muttering my name.

I blatantly let my eyes wander down his body. "So. Ten years later… Is it still so hard?"

He knows exactly what I'm referring to, and this time his laughter is rich and deep, putting us back on the familiar ground I was searching for.

When he doesn't answer, I poke again. "Getting *soft* in your old age?"

Ducking his head, Greg looks at me through his thick lashes. "You're not getting off the hook for this kiss. But if you want, I'll let you feel it first."

I bite my lip and he pulls his shirt from his trousers, raising the expensive fabric high enough to reveal the washboard abs he let me feel up after losing a bet on a Bulls game our senior year.

Maybe it's the night shadows playing tricks on me, but I don't think so. The bands of muscles wrapped tight across his abdomen look even bigger than they did when he was eighteen.

He takes my hand and presses it against the warm skin, and I yelp, pulling my hand back.

Eyes wide with disbelief, I look up into his amused face and then back to that rock-hard stomach, where my fingers have returned and are tentatively following the divides between the layers of muscle.

"Good lord, Greg, do you do crunches in your sleep?"

I start to crouch down, fascinated the same way I was in high school, because—

Big hands grip me beneath my arms, pulling me up again. "Show's over, Jules."

"Wait, one more—"

"Nope." He pushes me back against the support where I was leaning before and holds me there like he wants me to stay. "Enough putzing around."

At the lift of my brow, he rolls out his shoulders.

"Prepare to have your world rocked, to be ruined for all other dudes, or to fake all of the above for the sake of my fragile ego."

This time I'm the one who snorts. Greg's ego could shoulder the Sears Tower.

His hands come up to my face. It's a gentle touch, but more businesslike than seductive as he tilts my head just so. I was nervous before, but now… this feels like us.

"Can I keep touching your abs?"

A furrow digs between his brows. "No."

Dang it.

He gives me one last look, and for a split second, I'm not sure he's going to go through with it.

But then the corner of his mouth hitches the smallest degree, and he leans close. "Brace yourself, Jules."

# Chapter 4

*Greg*

*I* DON'T KNOW what I'm doing, acting like such a cocky fuck.

*Brace yourself.*

Right. Like one kiss from me, and Julia is going to need to reevaluate her whole life. Not likely.

But maybe the bravado is enough to distract her from the fact that I'm practically vibrating with the need to get my mouth on her. To taste her. Just once.

It was all fun and games until the moment I dipped her back and her eyes went soft and warm, sliding down to my mouth.

One glance, barely a second, and suddenly getting this kiss has become a critical thing.

I'm close enough to Julia that if our breathing syncs up, our chests will touch. Don't get me wrong—that would be fucking nice. But I'm not sure having all those lace-covered swells rub against my chest would be the best idea, so instead of closing the distance, I hold my ground, leaving that precarious inch of space between us.

I cup the sides of her face and look down at her mouth the way she'd looked at mine in the gym. Only instead of the fraction of a second it took for her to clear her eyes, I look my fill.

Ten years I've been waiting for this kiss, and something tells me that even if I wait another ten or ten after that, I'll never be this close again.

"Greg," she whispers, and those nerves I keep hearing in her voice before she says something outrageous are back.

But I don't want another joke. I don't want to lighten the mood.

I want to know what this kiss that's been flirting with me for the past ten years tastes like. So I take it.

Our kiss is sweet and soft and, because I don't want to rush past a single part, slow. Julia's mouth lives up to the hype. A closed-mouth kiss with that damned inch of space left between us ought to feel like a G-rated movie, but it's not. The supple give and gentle rub of her mouth against mine is up there with the dirtiest fantasies I've ever had.

Jesus, it feels like electricity is running through my veins.

Like my skin is on fire.

Like I want more.

I shouldn't push, because fuck, I don't want this to end. We didn't talk about boundaries. We didn't set a time limit or clarify where the lines are drawn. But if this is the only kiss I'm ever going to have from Julia… I want it to be *a kiss*. No holds barred. One for the books.

I sink in. Her lips part beneath mine on this startled little puff of breath that hits me harder than two hundred pounds coming across the ice at twenty miles an hour.

The hands I'd been so careful to keep gentle, firm. One slides deeper into her hair, the other cups the back of her neck.

I touch the pout of her bottom lip with my tongue and then slip into her mouth, taking that taste I've been so hungry for.

Damn, she's sweet and warm and soft, and when her tongue meets mine in a soft rub, I'm gone.

But then maybe so is she, because her hands aren't at her sides where I put them. They're tickling up my stomach, pressing flat against the abs that pure survival dictated I stop her from touching. That inch of space is gone, and I can't even remember why I thought keeping it was such a good idea.

Julia's curves and valleys pressed against me from thigh to chest are about the most perfect fucking thing in the world. Except now that I've had it, it isn't nearly enough. The hand in her hair tightens, and she moans, her fingers balling against my shirt as I urge her head back, opening her to more of my kiss.

Somewhere in the back of my brain there's a warning bell clanging, but by the time it filters through the taste of her tongue sliding against mine and the press of her hips, it might as well be one of those jingle bells our cat used to wear on his collar.

I'm no virgin, and when it comes to women, things have gotten hot and heavy more times than they haven't. But kissing Julia—it's different. I can't remember the last time I kissed like this. Hell, I can't remember ever kissing like this.

My mouth moves over her neck, and she angles her head to give me better access. That little moan of hers beside my ear has me trying to wrestle back the possessive-as-fuck high-school kid still residing deep inside me from sucking hard, putting my mark on her. That would be so hot—until she eviscerated me for it.

It might be worth the slow death.

We're burning out of control, and it's fucking amazing. Her arms are wrapped tight around my neck, her hands are in my hair, then moving over my shoulders and down to my abs and—Christ—she's got her fingers wrapped around my belt.

I freeze. It's only for a second, not even. Just long enough for my conscience to flash, "IS SHE GOING TO REGRET THIS?" on the Jumbotron in my brain. But before I have a chance to ask, her hands fly off my belt like it burned her, and I have my answer.

She would. Which means we won't.

As much as that kills me, I know it's for the best. This was only supposed to be a kiss.

So why am I thinking about getting her away from BHS and this reunion? Putting her in my car? Taking her back to my place so we can start making up for lost time?

"Jesus, Greg," she says with the kind of sharp laugh I'd have expected from her any time other than this. "You weren't kidding about the world-rocking quality of your kiss." Raising her fingers to her lips, she touches them tenderly and casts me a look that's a little accusing and a lot amused. That look has the power to yank me out of this weird space I ended up in and back to Julia and me and this kiss we saved up for, for ten years ultimately being nothing more than a joke.

*So make a fucking joke, numbnuts.*

"What can I say, Jules? I warned you."

"Yeah, but not that I was going to have to upgrade my vibrator." She looks back at me, shakes her head, and laughs, like she hasn't just planted the kind of visual I'm going to be playing with for the next ten years. "Quite a kisser, Greg."

"Good enough to earn me your promise for another at the next reunion?" Where the hell did that come from?

"Definitely." She says it like it's nothing. Like I haven't already marked my mental calendar and started counting down. "You ready to go back inside?"

Not even close. "You bet."

She runs her hands through her hair, and it looks like it did before I tangled it all up. A quick pinch at the side of her dress, and she's perfect.

"You going to tuck your shirt in there, stud, or are you planning to offer free feels when we get back inside?"

I don't even register what she's saying until she gives my shirt another pointed look and laughs. This is bad.

There's no clever comeback on the tip of my tongue, so I give up a chuckle and fix my shirt. "Good?"

Arching a brow at me, she steps closer. She stares at my hair, which is always a wreck, so I'm not exactly sure what damage she could have done out here, but once she slides her fingers through it a few times, I don't care.

Man, that's nice.

I'm about to step back when she moves down to my collar. She straightens my tie, flips down one of the points that somehow got turned up, and *closes the top button?*

"Sorry," she says, not looking very sorry at all.

When she gets to another open button about halfway down my chest, I'm the one raising a brow.

"Little handsy, there?"

"You're the one who needs the warning label."

"So this is my fault?" I scoff, but hell yes, I'll take full responsibility.

"Mmhmm. It is." Her lips pinch together, and even in the dim light, I can see her blush. "I'll let you get that last bit there."

I look down at where the tongue of my belt is partially free of the buckle and bark out a laugh. "Damn, Jules."

She turns farther away, letting out a huff. "I *said* I was sorry." Again with the whole not-sounding-very-sorry thing. Which I like a hell of a lot. Especially since the only thing I'm sorry about is that we stopped. And, well, that stopping was the right thing to do. Probably.

"I forgive you."

"Very big of you."

I grin, and she swats my arm, then gives it a little feel.

"Yeah, well it's only because hearing you're going to need a better vibrator just restocked my spank bank for the next year."

She laughs, and I rub the spot in the middle of my chest that's most affected by it.

"You're a pig."

"Yeah, but you like it." She always has, which is probably why I ramp up the bad behavior when she's around. I like the rise I get out of her. Hell, I like the rise she gets out of me.

Throwing an arm around her shoulders, I pull her into my chest and drop a quick kiss at the top of her head, falling back on the teasing banter that's been the foundation of our relationship for thirteen years. I'm mostly relieved by how easily it comes between us. Even if blowing off our actions doesn't feel completely right.

I rub my hands over her shoulders and step back before jutting my chin toward the reunion. It's time to get back.

She nods, stepping in with me. "Let's go."

When we get to the doors we came out of, she slows. "You go first. I'll make a call for work. If anyone happens to see me, it'll look less suspicious."

What the hell? I scan the dark corners around a building with too many shadows. "I'm not leaving you alone out here."

Her eyes go hard, and she crosses her arms. "Fine. I'll come inside, but I'll wait by the doors until you get around the corner."

"Yeah, where it's isolated enough for the two of us to sneak off for that—" Hell, *kiss* doesn't really seem sufficient, but Julia kind of circles her hand and nods like she gets where I'm coming from. "Jules, I know this is your hometown, but you don't really know these guys anymore. One of them could be a freak, waiting to catch you alone."

Her eyes soften. "You really are a sweet guy."

Catching her by the back of the elbow, I walk her inside. "I'm a belligerent ass who gets what he wants."

"Whatever you say."

She can ask my sister if she doesn't believe me.

We're close enough that I can hear voices from the

next hall. I pull out my phone and take a few steps away, holding it to my ear.

Julia does the same, and suddenly, we're just two people who can't let go of their careers for one night out with some old friends.

We return to the reunion, her first through the west doors, and then me, a few minutes later through the south.

We've gone our separate ways, but Julia stays on my radar. Ten minutes later, I catch her eyes when she's toasting with the girls she used to hang out with. Half an hour after that, I hear her laugh when she's surrounded by her old football team. And later still, I bring her a drink when she drops into a chair and slips off her heels. We get swept into a few groups together, laugh and talk about normal things, both of us doing a pretty decent job of acting like that kiss didn't happen. Mostly. Except for that single beat when our eyes hold longer than they should, and the temperature around us shoots up sixty degrees when her hand accidentally slides against mine.

Cost of doing business, I guess.

The reunion is winding down, and I'm taking pictures and signing a few autographs when I get her text.

**Julia: I'm beat. Heading out. Thanks for blowing my mind, rocking my world, ruining me for all other dudes, etc…**

Coughing into my hand, I scan the room and catch her at the door.

**Me: Looking forward to doing it again in ten years.**

She turns toward me, shaking her head like she still can't believe what we did. I can't quite believe it either.

Chapter 5

THE DOOR ISN'T even closed behind me when Cammy slides into the front hall of our apartment, her hands clasped in front of her. She's wearing leggings and an amorphous gray top, her blonde curls wadded up in a bun, an expectant gleam in her eyes.

"Did you do it? Tell me he kissed you. Ooh God, was it a dirty kiss? Greg looks *so* dirty. It's my favorite thing about him. Come on, did he?"

She's adorable, but being cute isn't going to save her after the stunt she pulled tonight.

I slide out of my heels and plant my hands on my hips. "I can't believe you sent that picture to Tabby." I most definitely can believe she went into my phone without my permission. Cammy's six years younger than I am, and she's never really grown out of that no-boundaries thing I thought was harmless when she was seven. "You know how I feel about that kind of press."

Rolling her eyes, she waves me off and grabs her own phone, her thumb moving at light speed over the screen. "The press is fine. Check this picture. It's the only one I've seen so far, but it is *awesome*!"

There on her phone is a picture from when Greg had me dipped back, his kiss squeaking in my ear. My eyes are bugged wide, my neck crunched at an angle that says I'm trying to get away from his nonsense. Most importantly, my hands are flared away from his body. It's funny and silly and nothing that's going to get me in trouble with anyone.

"That's the only one?"

She bounces on the balls of her sock-clad feet. "Why, was there more than one kiss? I know there was. There had to be. Wait, was it with someone else? No way. You wouldn't do that to Greg."

I never should have told her about the whole kiss business, but Cammy lives for this stuff. And even though she's only met Greg a few times, I must have talked about him enough to make a lasting impression, because the girl has an unwavering soft spot for him.

Encouraging her is probably a mistake, but then, how often does Cammy have something to get this excited about? Next to never, when it comes to my nonexistent love life. And even more rarely when it comes to her own. Being a single mother of a four-year-old boy when you're only twenty-two kind of cramps the dating life.

I tap my toe on the hardwood entry a couple of times, letting the suspense build, and then stroll into the kitchen. "Fine. Greg did kiss me, *privately*, and he was very good."

Cammy is on my heels in a flash, her hip pressing into mine as I stand at the sink and fill my glass from the tap. "And the dirty? Damn it, Julia, you know I've been stuck watching *Ask the Storybots* with Matty. I'm starved for the good stuff."

"What do you want to know?"

"Was there tongue? You're such a prude about dates… I bet there wasn't."

I know what she's doing, trying to bait me into giving her the details. Not like I wouldn't anyway, but now she's going to have to work for it. I let my lips curve into a secret smile, and she gasps, hand to her heart, stumbling back against the wall.

The drama. I'm laughing as I head to my bedroom.

"Oh my God, tongue! Wait, I don't want to get my hopes up here. Don't tease me, just give it to me straight. On the dirty scale of kisses, zero being that gross guy who worked as a TA while you were in school and had the bad breath and tooth sweaters."

"Joey."

"Right, Joey is a zero. And ten being the doctor from Manhattan. Craig something. With the clover tat on his butt."

"Kevin. And he was a pretty dirty kisser."

"Yeah, so Kevin's a ten. Where does Greg score? Eight? Nine? No, eight. I mean you're here, and I can see your panty line, so I know you're still wearing them. And FYI, I *told* you to skip the panties. What were you thinking in that dress?"

I twist around trying to see my butt in the closet mirror. "That I didn't want to show up at my reunion going commando? And for the record, the kiss with Greg was a seventeen. Panties and all." Though honestly, I'm surprised they weren't incinerated by how hot things got.

Cammy's eyes bug, and her mouth falls open, but before she can muster her next twenty questions, I shut myself into my bathroom.

Seventeen was way too conservative a number. Greg broke the dirty scale with that kiss. The way his tongue teased my mouth and those deep rumbling sounds coming from his chest while we kissed were more effective than any vibrator I've ever owned. But what got to me the most wasn't the clasp of his teeth on my lower lip or the flick of his tongue against the skin he'd just nipped… but the way his arms closed around me, holding me close and tight as he kissed me sense- less. That was the best part. Maybe the most alarming too, because that's the kind of kiss that puts dumb ideas in smart girls' heads.

I get into the shower to the sound of my sister knocking as quietly as possible, so as to not wake Matty, while whisper-yelling through the door. She has questions, but I want a few minutes to myself. To process. Maybe get my compartmentalization underway before I have to give up any more details about the kiss that blew my mind and the guy I can't start thinking of as anything more than my friend. But I'm not even through rinsing the shampoo from my hair when Cammy starts talking to me from the other side of the glass.

She picked the bathroom lock. Of course she did.

"Seventeen is a pretty outrageous number, coming from you. You're going to have to justify that score. Spare no details."

I ought to tell her to get out of the bathroom, but instead I clutch my shower loofah in front of me and start to spill.

When Cammy's questions are exhausted, I turn out the light and crawl into a bed that suddenly feels too big and imagine what it would be like if I weren't alone. If we hadn't stopped.

I blow out a shaky breath.

One night. That's how long I'll give myself to be wrapped up in Greg's kiss and think of my friend as more than that. One night to lie in bed and remember the feel of his hands tightening in my hair and his voice rumbling against my neck. One night to play at the edge of the riptide that is Greg's dirty-sweet kiss. I know it's dangerous, and I've already found myself too quickly swept away, but I can't quite put it aside. Not yet.

Sure, I put on my best face when we were done, made the requisite jokes to ensure he knew *I knew* nothing had changed. It was either that or launch myself at him and beg for more. And if I'm honest with myself, there was a moment where that was a close thing. Too close.

And if I'm being really, *really* honest, I kind of wish I could have justified more than one single kiss, because my sister is right. Greg looks like he'd be dirty. He talks like he'd be dirty. And he kisses like he'd be crazy dirty.

And with some pretty deep-seated trust issues with men in general, it's hard for me to let down my guard. So *dirty* isn't something I get a whole lot of in my life.

## Chapter 6

*Julia*

THE HALLS ARE bright, bustling with activity as everyone hustles to meetings, conference calls, or to catch whatever they've got cued up on their laptops. I'm in the office for a few hours to grab the last few games for both teams in this week's matchup and do some research on a couple stories I'll have ready in case I get tapped during the game.

"Julie, come on in here, will you?"

*Julie.* I cringe at the sound of Ray Hettler calling me as I pass his office. I don't work for him, but he treats me like I do. And sometimes the break between his department and mine gives him license to ask things I really wish he wouldn't ask.

I could keep walking and pretend I didn't hear him, but even though I don't report to him, the man holds some serious sway with the people I do report to, and I can't risk ticking him off.

Reluctantly, I backtrack and stop at his door.

"Afternoon, Ray. What's up?"

Ray's about thirty years older than I am, and I've learned the hard way not to ask what I can do for him because it either earns me the kind of suggestive leer that turns my stomach or has him asking me to grab him a cup of coffee or deliver paperwork to someone on a different floor. I'm a sideline reporter, not his girl Friday, but when I was first getting started, Ray was one of the guys who pulled for me when another candidate had already been picked.

"You're looking gorgeous as ever. Something new with your hair?" he asks, smoothing an unnaturally tanned hand over his sprayed dye job.

I shake my head and smile. Through all the years and all the games, never once has he stopped to compliment me on an interview. It's always about my appearance.

"Come on in a minute. Close the door behind you."

The alarms start to blare in my head, but I can't really say no without risking him flying off the handle, something everyone has seen at least once or twice. I catch a pitying look from the mail guy as he pushes his cart, but I've got this. It's not like we're the last people on the floor at the end of the night.

I close the door and take a deep breath. "Ray, if

this is about the photo that's circulating from this weekend, it was nothing."

"Nothing? It looked like one hell of a good time. Quite the party." He swipes his tablet to life and shows me the picture on the screen. "Couple kids, cutting loose. No responsibilities for the night. Anything can happen."

My spine goes rigid.

A couple kids. That's what we look like. Maybe not to everyone, maybe not even to Ray, but he's right. To some, this picture, like the incident with the man captured in it, needs to be an exception to the rule. I need to be viewed as a woman responsible enough to be trusted with reporting on the game… not some party girl with zero credibility.

"I understand perceptions and the kind of impression this could give. I'll be more careful about my public image."

"Maturity, Julie. Responsibility. Security. That's what you want to reinforce. Show them how grounded you are."

"Absolutely."

He nods, cracking a smile. "It certainly does look fun though. And the hockey player?"

"Old friend, is all." An old friend with a mouth more addictive than crack cocaine and apparently just as dangerous. This conversation is exactly why I need to stop thinking about him.

"Be careful there. People will be watching now."

Ray sets the tablet aside on his desk, then turns back and, giving me a not-too-subtle once-over, lets out a low whistle through his teeth. As though that were some appropriate segue, he waves to the cluster of low chairs and a sofa deeper into his office, suggesting we sit.

He's been hearing good things about me lately. There's talk about a new show, and my name's been thrown around for the job.

I've heard some of what he's saying from my agent before. We've been strategizing on where my career can go next, and she's got feelers out everywhere. But some of what he's saying, I haven't heard.

"Julie, you're almost there." He sets his hand on my knee, and the breath stops in my chest. "You need the right people to keep saying the right things, but then it's going to happen."

---

"AND THEN HE ASKED YOU OUT?" Cammy gasps, her hands balled on her hips. Lowering her voice, she glances past me to the living room where Matty sits cross-legged, his little head of blond curls bowed over the Lego fortress he's erecting. "What an epic douche. How'd you get out of it?"

Carefully. "First, he didn't ask me out on a date, per se. He proposed getting together at his place in Florida for a few days to discuss opportunities for my future."

She starts walking toward the kitchen and bends to

sweep up a stray action figure on the way. "Right, so you could see what you could do for each other. Barf."

I laugh, but the very fact that I have enough experience to be able to take this sort of thing in stride is depressing as hell.

"I basically reminded him about my very strict policy of not dating—or even giving people reason to suspect I might be dating—anyone from the industry." There's an open bottle of white in the fridge and I pour us both a glass. "And while *I know* what he's suggesting would be on the up-and-up, I couldn't risk the perception that there was something else going on."

"You know I'm not the biggest fan of that rule, but it has come in handy from time to time."

"It has." It protects Ray's bloated ego, keeping him from turning on me. The guy is an ass, but the last thing I need is a good old boy like him as an enemy.

I take a sip of wine and relax into the counter behind me.

Cammy picks at her thumbnail. "Do you feel better after talking about it?"

"Umm… sure."

Her smile bursts free, and she leans forward, eyes wide. "So, any chance you heard from Mr. Dirty Kisser today?"

*Greg*

THE LOCKER ROOM IS LOUD, with blaring music and half the guys talking over each other. The other half are laughing their asses off, tossing bills at Rux's feet as he works his hairy-as-fuck body in this hip-thrusting stripper dance, wearing his jock and nothing else. I ought to be pouring a bottle of water on his chest or some shit, but instead my inner fifteen-year-old girl is stuck staring at my phone. Martin, one of the guys I reconnected with at the reunion, is throwing a party tonight and invited me to come.

My living depends on my ability to make solid decisions in fractions of a second. But I've been staring at this invite for a full five minutes already, trying to decide what the fuck to do. Knowing whatever I choose isn't going to have jack to do with Martin, who's a seriously cool guy, even if he did used to play football. It's about Julia… because she's pretty good friends with him too. Which means there's a chance she'll be there. And while the man downstairs is already starting to primp, I'm not entirely sure seeing her again so soon is a good thing.

It's been a week since the reunion.

I've texted her, of course.

We're friends. It would be shitty not to.

But no matter how easy her reply was, it feels different to me. She's in my head, and even after playing three games this week, I'm not any closer to getting her out.

That's not how it's supposed to be with her.

Rux grabs the side of my breezers and starts using me like a pole. "Dude, what's on the phone. A bunny send you another picture of her tits? Lemme see."

Hell. I toss my phone back on the shelf and straight-arm his chest. "No dirty pictures, so you can stop humping me."

He stumbles back, nearly stepping on Vsev, who's down picking up the dollars. "But you're so big and strong."

He's a laugh riot, but this thing with Jules is really bugging me.

"You ever get caught up with a woman you know better about?"

He raises a brow. "Like a bunny?"

Bunny? Fuck no. Not even a little bit.

But then I stop and think, because putting aside the fact that Julia is essentially the antithesis of a puck bunny, the situation isn't that far off. Both are attractive women I know better than to get serious about, and both could be filed under: *Exception to the rule*.

"Not exactly, but close enough." Saying it makes my gut feel wrong.

"Who you been doing?" he demands, beefy arms stacked behind his matted brown curls as he does a few more Magic Mike thrusts.

"Doesn't matter, because it's not something that'll happen again."

Rux's tone turns serious and his arms drop to his sides. "Dude. It matters. I don't want to be your *Eskimo brother.*" At my very-not-amused look, he shrugs. "So what, you hooked up with someone you don't want to get serious with, but you want to hit it again?"

"No. That's not it." Jesus, why did I think talking to this guy was a good idea? "I—fuck, I keep thinking about her, even though I shouldn't want her that way."

Because we're friends and all that shit.

"Ah, easy then. Wait 'til you see her again. If you aren't into this thing goin' anywhere, one look and your ass'll be straightened out." He shakes his head. "You're not the type to nail her just 'cause you can."

He's right. I'm not. At least not anymore.

"Hey, wanna hit a club tonight?"

I clap him on the shoulder and start getting dressed. "Can't. Got a party I'm going to."

---

*Julia*

ONE NIGHT. Twelve hours. That's what I gave myself. And considering I don't normally waste twelve minutes on the guys who threaten my rules, that was pretty generous. So what the heck am I doing standing in the middle of Martin's party a full week later, wondering what Greg Baxter is doing tonight? He's not playing a game. They wiped up the ice with the Lightning last night, and tonight they're off.

Maybe he's with the team. He once told me that

most nights, he'd rather hang out at one of the guys' houses than let Rux drag him around to a club. I wonder if they invited a few girls over.

My belly tenses at the thought and, recognizing the pang of misplaced jealousy for what it is, I cough out a laugh.

Sarah or Sidney or whatever the name of the woman I'm standing with stops talking, and my cheeks start to burn.

"Sorry, frog in my throat. I'm fine. Go on."

I am so *not* fine.

Jealous? Absolutely not. I don't get jealous. Ever. I don't get invested enough to merit that kind of emotion. And to get jealous over Greg Baxter? No. We're friends with one little kiss between us. One exceptionally dirty, scorchingly hot kiss with the staying power to wreck my brain for the better part of a week.

Like I need *that* again.

I refocus on the woman in front of me and accept a refill on my wine when Martin's girlfriend Dana comes around with a bottle. I keep waiting to see a ring on her finger, because this girl is a keeper, and that's not just wishful thinking on my part. It's in every look Martin gives her. He's the kind of guy that will stick around too.

Dana asks *Simone*—thank God I didn't call her Sarah—about the work she's having done on her condo, and suddenly the conversation I was only marginally following makes more sense. This is ridiculous. Listening to people is my job. Even if it wasn't, I like to think I'm more considerate than this.

The conversation turns from one topic to another. Simone excuses herself, and another couple joins us for a few minutes before moving on. Dana has me in stitches as she recounts Martin's kitchen-related quirks. Hard to believe this is the same man who set his mom's microwave on fire junior year trying to make mac and cheese. I'm about to say as much when the air seems to shift, and the cacophony of party sounds dull.

My mouth closes, and I turn toward the entry where the guests have been arriving in a steady stream. It's him. Greg. I have to blink to make sure he's actually there and not some figment of my imagination, too easily conjured after the way he's been on my mind this week. But in the next second his blazing blue eyes come up, they connect with mine, and his mouth tips into a cocky slant even my imagination couldn't get right.

My heart starts to pound and—God, are my hands shaking?

I can't believe he's here.

*Why* is he here?

That's a silly question. Martin invited him after catching up at the reunion.

Greg isn't mine alone. He isn't mine at all.

Dana touches my shoulder. "Martin's flagging me from the kitchen. Give me a few minutes."

I nod and she gives me a quick squeeze, but my attention is on the tallest man in the room as he cuts through the party… heading for me. Perfectly worn denim moves around his heavily muscled legs, and a cream sweater pushed up his forearms stretches over the solid definition of his shoulders and chest. No man should look this good. He's halfway through the crowd when a couple of guys step into his path, drawing his attention until our eye contact breaks.

The breath leaves my lungs in a rush. I turn away, my nerves going haywire. It's just Greg, only he hasn't felt like *just Greg* since last week. And the look in his eyes when he saw me—it's different from the way he's looked at me before.

I think.

Maybe it's me.

Scanning the room, I search for a friendly face. Someone to pull into conversation and serve as a buffer between us.

Greg's hand meets my shoulder. It's warm and wide and feels like it's feeding that low charge that's been running through me since the minute his mouth met mine.

"Julia."

We're friends. I can do this.

"Hey stranger," I say, turning back to him with a practiced smile.

His brows furrow like he doesn't know what to make of my reaction. I hardly know what to make of it myself.

"Was wondering if I'd see you here." He rubs the

back of his neck. "Funny how seldom our paths actually cross when we've been living in the same city for over a year now."

I make a dismissive sound, waving my hand away even though I know he's right. It's the nature of our jobs. I'm on the road three days a week minimum for the games I cover, and Greg's schedule is even more nuts. "We text."

"Talk on the phone a few minutes here and there." He bites his bottom lip. "We don't see enough of each other though."

If he'd brought this up a week ago, I wouldn't have thought a thing about it except that he was right.

He leans closer. "Why don't we hang out more?"

I'm saved from answering when a couple of Martin's cousins come up and introduce themselves. I've met these guys before, but they're clearly here for Greg. In the past I've felt possessive of my time with him, because he's right, we don't see enough of each other. But now, I'm grateful for the reprieve. The guys want to rehash last night's game, and Greg accommodates them for a few minutes, answering questions, listening to their analysis. But every time his heated eyes meet mine, linger and hold for a second, the tension between us builds that much more.

It's getting hard to breathe, hard for me to think about anything beyond how good it felt to be beneath his kiss, and whether it would be like that again.

Maybe I was just hard up.

Like it's been so long since I had any quality lip action, I'm blowing things out of proportion. Making that one kiss with Greg into more than it actually was.

Heck, if he kissed me again, it might be a total letdown. I hazard a look at his face and find his eyes on me again. A tremor runs through me.

Or maybe it wouldn't be a letdown.

Someone asks Greg about what it's like knowing he might be traded to a different team and have to move at the drop of a hat.

I hear his voice, but what he's saying fades when I feel the brush of his hand against mine. It's barely contact, the backs of his fingers. It's the type of touch that could be seen as completely accidental, but this isn't. This is deliberate.

And it sets a dozen butterflies to flight in my belly.

Greg smudged the line again, and my facade of cool is going to crack if I don't put some distance between us.

"Excuse me for a minute, will you guys?"

I don't dare look, but I can feel Greg's eyes on me with every retreating step I take. When I get to the hall bathroom, there are a couple of women waiting ahead of me. Then, like an angel of mercy, Dana comes around the corner and, seeing the line, grabs my arm and points me toward the far end of the apartment. "You look like you could use a minute. Martin's office has a bathroom off it. We never use it, so forgive the mess, but take all the time you need."

She's officially one of my favorite people tonight. "Thank you, Dana."

When I reach the office, it's filled with boxes still labeled from their move two years ago. That's very much the Martin I know. Then, that good humor fades as the quiet settles around me and I ask myself what I'm doing.

Greg is one of my oldest friends. An athlete with ties to an industry I've made it my goal to conquer. I can't get breathless every time our eyes meet. I can't keep thinking about what it was like when he kissed me or how no one I've dated before was capable of making me feel that way.

I can't.

The latch from the door closing sounds behind me, and I know it's him. I should feel frustration, but it's relief that washes over me when I turn to find him there. His hair is standing up in different directions, like maybe he's shoved his hands through it since I left him three minutes ago. But it's his eyes I can't look away from. The laughter I usually find in those gorgeous blues is gone, and all that's left is heat.

## Chapter 7

*Greg*

SO THAT PLAN is shot to hell.

One look at Julia and I'm worse off than I was a week ago. She's fucking gorgeous. And while that's been the case since the day I met her, I'm seeing something different now. I'm seeing more than the surface-level assortment of attractive features, more than the brash friend I've been joking around with for thirteen years. I'm seeing the soul-deep sensuality Julia so effectively hides from everyone else, the passion and playfulness. I'm seeing the vulnerability she won't admit to and a need that mirrors my own.

I'm seeing potential for something bigger than what we already are to each other.

And now that I've seen it, I don't want to pretend I haven't.

"You wouldn't be running away from me, would you, Jules?"

"What? No. I…" Her cheeks take on a warm glow, and she smooths a nonexistent wrinkle from the burgundy dress that wraps around her in a phenomenal way.

"You were running." I move closer. "So the question is… were you running because you wanted me to chase you?"

Her eyes snap up, pupils wide. I step even closer, and yeah, that look is telling me two things. One, she definitely likes the idea of me chasing her. And two, she'll never admit it.

"All I want is for things to be the way they always have with us. I want us to be friends."

"We are friends." Friends on the brink of being something more.

She crosses to the desk covered with boxes. "*Just* friends."

A few hours ago, getting friend-zoned was exactly what I wanted. Or thought I wanted, anyway. But now?

I rub the back of my neck. "Yeah, about that *just*."

Her head drops forward into a low shake, but not before I see the smile I'd been hoping for.

"*Greg.*"

This is my Julia, scolding me with a smile on her face and laughter in her eyes. This is the woman I can talk to about anything.

"Come on, Jules, tell me you haven't been thinking

about it. Tell me you haven't been wondering what it would have been like if we hadn't stopped when we did. If at the end of the night you'd come home with me."

It doesn't matter what she says. I can see in her eyes she's been thinking about it as much as I have. Like I can see that as much as she might want to put that *just* back between us, there's a bigger part of her that doesn't. *Just* friends don't stare at each other's mouths when they talk, they don't bite their lips when their eyes drop lower than that.

"*Julia*."

Guilty eyes snap back to mine, and she huffs. "Fine, yes. Of course I've been thinking about it. But honestly, I've been in a bit of a dry spell. So, you know, it's not about us."

Dry spell? Finding the edge of the desk, I lean back and cross my arms. "This I've got to hear."

"Don't get your ego in a bunch. The kiss was good."

"Mind-blowing, world-rocking, etcetera…" Distinctions are important.

She rolls her eyes and walks past me. It takes everything I have not to pull her into my arms right then.

"But this whole sort of extended obsession thing probably has more to do with my not getting out that much than—than anything else."

Running my hand over my mouth, I wipe away the smile trying to fight free. She said *obsession*. Things are definitely looking up. "You're saying if we kissed again, it wouldn't be as good."

"It wouldn't be *bad*," she adds in a rush, like she's worried about my feelings being hurt.

"Right. But nothing you couldn't walk away from."

"Greg, don't take it personally. I can walk away from pretty much anything."

We'll see about that. "Great, then it's settled."

Her eyes narrow. "What is?"

"We'll kiss again." I push off the desk and start toward her at the opposite wall. Slowly. "So you can stop *obsessing*."

She looks a little nervous now, her posture stiffening as she follows my steps with her eyes. "Obsessing is probably too strong a word. I really don't think—"

"Consider it a favor from me to you."

"A *favor*?" she coughs out. "Please."

Damn, I love firing her up.

"Yeah." I round the couch piled with magazines and she takes a step back. "Don't worry. When I kiss you again, Julia, I won't go easy." Her breath hitches. "Rest assured, I'm going to give it everything I have— so there's no doubt in your mind when we're done. You'll be able to walk away confident the only thing behind that obsessing was a dry spell that's now been quenched."

Her back meets the wall, and I brace my hand above her head, taking in the darkening of her eyes and the quickening of her breath. "Sound like a good plan?"

She nods.

Leaning in even closer, so I can smell her perfume and feel the tickle of her hair at my jaw, I whisper, "You know there's a flaw in your logic, right?"

"W-what?"

Not so confident now.

"You may not get out much, but what's *my excuse*, Jules? Because I get out plenty, and I haven't been able to stop thinking about the taste of your kiss from the first minute I had to give it up." I run my nose against the shell of her ear, reveling in the unmistakable tremor that follows. "All I can think about is your mouth and everything I want to do with it."

Her breath comes out in a warm rush, leaving her lips parted in the most tempting way. I bring my thumb to that soft, padded swell and then trace it down the pretty line of her neck in a path I want to follow with my tongue.

"Greg," she says weakly, "you're not playing fair."

I'm playing the only way I know how. *To win.*

"No? We could stop." I say to see her reaction. To make sure I'm not letting my ego get ahead of me and misreading something that's important to me on a vital level.

"We could," she acknowledges softly, her eyes never leaving my mouth.

Yeah, I don't think so. "But really, what's one more kiss?"

Her nod is so small it's almost imperceptible. That's something about Julia. You have to look really hard to see what's going on inside her head. More than that, you need to know what to look for.

And I do.

"Between friends," she whispers before we collide.

Our first kiss beneath the bleachers started out slow and careful, and stopped at the edge of control. This kiss begins there. Julia meets me with a moan, her mouth open to the thrust of my tongue. Our hands are everywhere, moving in an urgent quest for more contact.

Her body is perfect, the curve of her hips a perfect fit to my flexing fingers, her breasts full and soft against my chest in a firm press. Her head is thrown back and my mouth is moving down the sexy column of her neck. Jesus, she smells good. I give in and lick the shadowy hollow between her breasts.

"Damn you," she gasps, her fingers sliding into my hair and gripping tight.

"Dry spell, my ass."

Then I'm kissing her again. Harder. Faster. It's hot and frantic and fucking amazing.

Her body bows beneath the bend of mine, and the feel of her that way is like a drug. I want more. My arms snake around her, one at her waist and one across her ass, pulling her into closer contact until our hips are flush and that stretchy flowy skirt she's wearing rises as her knee skims higher up my thigh.

I can't believe this is Julia. My Julia.

I mean, I'm a guy, and she's fucking amazing, so yeah, I've thought of her like this over the years. Joked about it. But we're friends, and that means a hell of a lot to me, so I never expected to act on it. But now, all the little ways she's stood apart from the crowd are starting to come together in a way that's new and hot, and filled with so much fucking potential, I can't believe I didn't see it before.

We're rocking together, me against her belly, her against my thigh, and the little sounds she's making, damn, they're sexy.

Her knee is hitched at my hip, her skirt bunched high and her shoulders against the wall. I smooth my hand up the toned line of her leg to the edge of her panties and then over them, groaning at the damp heat. When she rocks into my touch and gives me the softest, neediest little cry I've ever heard, something inside me snaps.

I fist her panties, and a second later, they're off her body, the torn remnants sliding into my pocket for safe-keeping. Julia's eyes go wide, her lips parting on a rush of breath that tells me she very much likes the liberty I just took.

"I've got to touch you, Jules." It's my only defense.

She blinks up at me, cheeks flushed, pupils blown wide. That look. I'll never forget it. Never get enough of it. Grabbing my hair, she pulls me back into her kiss and moans around the thrust of my tongue as my fingers slide through her pussy. Slick and wet.

She's going to be the end of me.

I'm not going to fuck her, though. Not here in some cluttered back room at a friend's party. But I also can't stop. Not yet.

"Greg," she gasps as I play between her legs, following her slit from one end to the other, stopping to circle her clit before sliding one finger in for a shallow tease.

"So tight." I think about her dry spell and wonder how long it's been. But then I shove that thought away because I don't want to think about anyone being here but me, no matter how long it's been. "So wet, Jules. Is all this for me?"

She doesn't have a chance to answer before I sink deep, wanting her to feel me in places neither of us ever thought I'd get.

I tell her how hot she is, what she's doing to me. What I want to do to her. And when I kiss her again, it's hard. Demanding.

My tongue matches the strokes of my finger, in and out, firm and deep. She's humming around me. I can taste how close she is, feel it in the greedy grasp around my finger.

Tearing away from the claim I've staked on her mouth, I move to her ear. "I need to hear you come. I need to know what you sound like *coming for me*."

Her eyes fly to mine, and that contact hits me like lightning. Too fast to realize what's coming or prepare for the shock.

*Julia.*

I've looked into those honeyed pools too many times to count, but she's never let me see past the playful edge. She's never let me into this soulful, secret place that's about the most beautiful thing I've ever seen.

I don't want to blink, can't risk breaking something I'm not sure she'll let me have again. Something I don't want to give up.

"Kiss me, Greg," she whispers, and I give her what she wants, sinking into the slowest, deepest, most soul-fucking-shattering kiss of my life. Another beckoning stroke within her wet heat, and she shatters, clinging to me as I swallow her cries, kiss her breathless, and wring every last bit of pleasure from her there is.

I slip my hand from between her legs and, after a last appreciative caress, release her knee to slide down my thigh.

Distantly I register that we're still at a party with barely more privacy than we had beneath the bleachers.

I should take her out of here. Take her home. Take her… well, anywhere.

She's still leaning against the wall, her dress caught halfway up her thighs and twisted across her chest so it's barely covering the breast I helped myself to however many minutes ago. But it's her eyes that give her away. Heavy-lidded and soft-focused, she looks like a walking advertisement for back-room nookie.

It's a far cry from the controlled image she maintained at the reunion, and it feels like a victory of the chest-thumping variety to me. But it's nothing I want anyone else to see. This look is *mine*.

"Here, let me." I start at the top, smoothing her hair as best I can before moving on to where her dress vees in front and the skewed bra beneath.

"I can get that." She's still a little breathless, her voice not entirely steady. "Just give me a minute."

"Pretty sure I owe you a put-together after last time."

She reaches up and gently touches the corner of my mouth, smiling.

"What?"

"You've got a dirty mouth."

My grin cranks up. "Are you surprised?"

"Not at all."

Her skirt is still exposing her toned legs, and I can't bring myself to fix it yet. I lean in again, tipping her chin to my kiss.

The temptation to get lost in it again is strong, but instead I pull back and meet her eyes.

"Let's get out of here."

*Julia*

*Get out of here?*

I just came harder than I have in my whole life, and he wants to leave before I have a chance to repay the favor? "What—umm—what about you?"

"Don't worry about me. We'll get a car." Greg's hand is warm against my cheek, his eyes tender as they search mine. Too tender. "I'll buy you an ice cream. A drink. Something."

"Like a date?" I rest my hand against his chest and give up a gentle laugh.

*I don't date athletes.* But even if I did, that's not what this was about.

"Look, I get it, Greg. We're friends, and you're probably trying to make sure I don't feel cheap or used or whatever. But you don't need to worry. I *wanted* this." It's so true, I have to look away as I mutter, "In case you couldn't tell."

He ducks his head, invading my vision again. Heavy angles and hard lines add to the collection of roughhewn features that make up the most beautiful face I know. There's nothing gloating or smug in his tone when he says, "I could tell. And I think it's pretty safe to say we've established the whole world-rocking thing is specific to us and can't be attributed to any dry spells. Which is why you ought to break your rule for me."

The way he's looking at me has me closer to

agreeing than I've ever been before, except— "I don't break my rule for anyone."

His brows knit together as my words sink in. "*Julia.*"

"No." I sigh and push off the wall, half surprised to find my legs actually holding me. "Look, I know that was… *intense*. Obviously after all these years, that IOU had some heavy interest on it."

"You aren't seriously going to try and sell me on this again."

"Yes, I'm going to try and sell you on this." Absolutely, I am. I can't afford to get caught up in the idea that there's something special or significant between us. I don't date athletes and Greg Baxter is top-tier. "Fine, I wasn't expecting that kind of chemistry. But the chemistry doesn't have to be an issue. I mean seriously, thirteen years of friendship. You don't really want to risk it on a few sparks."

I know I don't. Especially considering Greg's track record with women. He's a player. Even back in high school, I can't remember him going more than a week or two with the same girl before moving on. And yeah, some of that was because there wasn't room for much in his life beyond hockey, but still. I see the tabloids. I know his reputation. In ten years, not much has changed.

All that aside, I don't want to risk the professional credibility I've worked so hard to establish.

"A few sparks?" He stalks away and then turns to

come back. "Julia, have you ever felt anything like that?"

Never. Not once in my life.

"What does it matter? We're friends!"

His mouth slides into a familiar half-smile, but it doesn't match his eyes. "Yeah, friends who burn inferno hot when their mouths touch."

My confidence falters, but I don't let it show. "Okay, but deep down, we're still friends before anything else, right? Good enough friends that we should know better than to try and make more of this than it is. I don't want to mess things up. And what about my job? I can't, Greg."

He stares at me, eyes hard and intense. I don't know what he's thinking, but I have the distinct impression I'm getting a look at what the opposing center sees during a face-off. It's disconcerting, but in a blink, it's gone.

"Okay." He ducks his head, rubbing the back of his neck. When he looks back at me, it's with the carefree smile I've been counting on for as many years as we've been friends. "So friends?"

Really? Just like that?

Greg's always been a guy who burned hot and cold, but still, that was fast. Not that I'm complaining.

"Always."

As if on cue, his pocket starts to vibrate, and with a last look he takes a step back and answers the call with a terse, "Yeah?"

The little bubble of intimacy we shared pops, and I feel colder. But I know I'm right.

Greg shoves a hand through the sexy mess of his hair and turns, signaling for me to wait a minute. "Thanks, man. Yeah, I'm getting out of here pretty quick anyway… you too."

"What's going on?"

Pocketing the phone, he walks over to the window and glances out. "Someone posted we're here."

Instantly I'm on alert.

"I don't see any press out front, but that's probably going to change pretty quick." He turns, squinting back at me. "I'm not really in the mood for sound bites and smiling for the cameras tonight. You going to stay or go?"

The two of us leaving at the same time would be suspect. I need to play it smart.

"I'll stay. You go." Heat pushes into my cheeks, and I nod toward his fly. "I'm sorry about—"

He cuts me off with a laugh and, wrapping his big hand around my shoulder, leans in to drop a quick kiss on the top of my head. A *friendly* kiss.

"Don't worry about it." Flashing a wink that's pure Baxter, he adds, "Gives me something to take home to *Keri*."

I burst out laughing as he cuts toward the door. *Keri*. The hand lotion he's been referencing as his significant other since high school. "Have fun."

"I will… Say, Jules, you get around to upgrading

that vibrator yet?"

This guy. "No," I laugh out, because only Greg could throw that in like it's casual conversation.

He flashes me a wicked wink. "Want to make sure I'm working with an accurate visual for later. Night, Jules." The door closes behind him, and I slump into the only chair in the room not stacked with boxes.

We're good.

This is what I want. And that gnawing feeling in the pit of my stomach—the one that has a lot to do with the look in Greg's eyes when he asked me to break my rules for him—well, it'll go away.

Two hours later, I'm home in bed when I get Greg's text with a picture of a box of tissues, a candle, rose petals, a twenty-ounce water, and his pump-bottle of lotion… all I can do is laugh. Until I stop laughing, because now I'm thinking about it. About the thick, long fingers that had been so deep inside me… wrapped around *him*.

My thighs squeeze together, and I try not to dwell on the way he kissed me or the rumble of his voice when he told me he needed to hear me come. But it's too late. My eyes are sliding closed as my hands inch between my legs to my still-swollen sex.

I shouldn't.

I won't.

I—

Another text. The tissue box. Empty and on its side. *That man!*

## Chapter 8

*Julia*

FIVE MILES ON the treadmill should have been enough to get my head straight, but by the time I stumble off my machine, all I've accomplished is muscles that burn so bad I can barely walk, and I end up having to hail a cab for the three-block trip back to my place.

I can't believe I let it happen again. Greg gave me every opportunity to stop him last night, but by the time his mouth finally met mine, I was shaking with need. It didn't matter that we were at Martin's party, that anyone could have noticed we'd disappeared into a locked room together, or that I'd sworn there wouldn't be any repeats of the kiss from the reunion. All that mattered was the way he looked at me and how every crooked smile pulled me that much further past the lines I'd drawn in the sand. By the time my shoulders hit the wall, I would have grabbed hold of any excuse Greg offered to justify what had become inevitable.

The elevator doors slide open with a ding, and I push off the rail, trying to shake the sensual fog clouding my mind with dirty kisses and even dirtier talk.

Why did he have to ask for more?

If he'd pulled away from that kiss and held up his hand for a parting high-five, we both could have walked out of that room without a care in the world. But instead, I'm swamped with all these *what if*s and *wouldn't it be nice*s and *maybe in another life*… because in this one, what Greg was offering just isn't in the cards.

At least he saw reason in the end.

I let myself into the apartment and drop my keys into the catchall as Matty slides into the room in a padded Superman muscle suit and two paper plates fashioned into slippers.

"AJ, you got a package!" he shouts, flinging himself at my legs and then wiggling to get free when I crouch down for a full-size hug.

Matty's been calling me AJ since his first words and couldn't manage the mouthful "Aunt Julia" made. It started as a little slurring of sounds about a month after he nailed "Mama," and Cammy and I thought it was so cute and, since it made sense, we went with it.

"Hey there, Superman. How was your day?"

"Good. I had applesauce *twice*! Is the package for me? Mommy says it's not for me, but I bet it is."

I think back, trying to remember what I've ordered. There were the mittens that matched Cammy's coat, but they weren't supposed to be here for another week or so.

"I'm not sure, little man. Maybe you can help me open it and we'll find out who it's for together."

"Yes!"

He darts off toward the kitchen, and I follow, checking my phone. I've got seventeen texts from the hour and a half I've been at the gym. I've cleared four of them when I see the next one is from Greg.

Matty's voice carries around the corner. "She *said* I could open it!"

Cammy replies, but I can't make out what she's saying.

**Greg: For when you're thinking of me.**

My brow furrows and then the penny drops. My feet are already moving as I belt out, "Cammy, no! Do not open that box. Matty, let AJ pick out a present for you instead. Don't open it!"

I skid around the corner and find Matty kneeling on a chair at the kitchen table and Cammy by the sink, both staring at me like I've grown a second head. The package in question is parked on the counter, untouched.

Heart slamming, I collapse against the door frame.

"AJ, are you okay?" Matty asks as his mother steps over and rubs a hand over his tiny back.

"Yeah, Aunt Julia, you're looking a little *funny*."

I nod and then nod again. Everything is fine. Except I have the feeling I might need to murder Greg Baxter.

"I'm going to grab this box and take it back to my room."

Cammy's eyes narrow on the box in question and then shift back to me. "Why? What's in the box, Jules?"

My lips purse together, and I inch toward the opposite counter. "N-nothing important." That might have sounded more believable without the guilty-sounding stutter.

I grab the box and dart to my room, almost getting the door closed behind me before Cammy stuffs the full length of her arm through. There's no choice but to let her in.

Next thing I know, she's snatched the box out of my hands and is bouncing on my bed, giving it a solid shake.

"Spit it out. I've got Matty counting macaroni noodles to make dinner, but he's four. He can't count that high."

"I think it's from Greg."

Her mouth forms a perfect O, and she slowly lifts the box to her ear and gives it a gentle shake. "What is it?"

I've got a guess, but I can't bring myself to actually say.

My expression must be telling enough, because now she's tearing at the Prime packing tape and ripping through the cardboard until the box lies open on the bed between us.

"No way," she gasps in stunned awe.

But yes. Greg Baxter sent me a vibrator.

Blinking up at me, she whispers, "I kind of love him."

That makes two of us. But as a *friend*, and with all the necessary disclaimers.

---

*Greg*

**JULIA: Got your present.**

I'm feeling pretty smug about it until I see the accompanying picture of some tiny kid with loopy blond curls and a superhero costume staring down at a torn-open shipping box, a confused look on his innocent face.

"Oh shit," I croak out, my gut churning. Rux shoots me a curious glance from where he's sprawled on his seat, but I wave him off.

We're on the tarmac with a few minutes left before takeoff for San Jose, so I call her.

She answers on the first ring and I dive straight into my grovel.

"I am so sorry. Jules, you gotta believe me, I never would have sent it if I'd thought Matty would see it." What kind of kid opens his aunt's mail? Maybe they all do. Shit, I need to learn more about kids. Talk about how *not* to get the girl. "I'm sorry. If he needs therapy or a specialist or something, I'll pay for it. For Cammy, too."

I'm ready to pop for a private school education when I hear her muffled cry through the line. It feels like something inside of me died.

"God, please, Julia. Don't cry."

But then I hear it again, more clearly, and that's no cry at all.

"Are you *laughing*?" I demand, because it sure as hell sounds like she is.

"Greg, you totally deserve that!"

"He didn't open the box?" *Please say he didn't.* I try to be a decent guy, especially when it comes to kids.

"We let him open it, but only after we'd replaced the contents with a bag of frozen peas."

I breathe easier and relax into my chair as the sound of Julia's laughter warms me. She's going to pay for that stunt, but for now I'm enjoying this moment.

"I figured that box had to be staged. It looked like a couple of wolves tore into it going after a slab of meat inside."

"Believe it or not, that was Cammy. She gets excited."

"Cammy opened it?" The guilt's back as I think about how I would feel if *my* little sister opened a package like that. *Gah*. Don't think about it. Don't.

"Matty I can control. His mother, not so much." There's some noise from the background, and then Julia is back, a smile in her voice. "By the way, I think you made her whole year."

"How about yours?"

Our attendant Vicky is walking through the aisle, motioning that we're about to take off. I signal for one more minute as Julia's voice comes through the line. "Too early to say, but I'll let you know."

I grab a magazine and lay it over my lap to cover the semi I'm sporting.

Score one for Julia.


WE KICK ass in the Shark Tank and a few hours later hop back on the plane to Arizona for a game against the Coyotes. I text Julia the next morning after watching video from the last game with the coaches, asking if she's got anything to report. I've been thinking about her pretty much nonstop the last few days. A lot of it's dirty... her head thrown back and her hands between her legs as she plays with the toy I sent. I want to know how far-off my fantasies are... if she was thinking of me, but all I get back are some bullshit football stats she probably collected for the game she's covering tomorrow night. Rux catches me grinning at my phone and wants to know what's up, but for as much as I share with him, I'm keeping this close to my chest. At least for now.

We're back in Chicago the next day, but Julia's in Oakland, so I'm SOL for any *accidental* run-ins with her. Maybe that's not the worst thing. I'm not exactly a patient guy, and Julia's not ready to accept what's going on with us. Yet. She needs some time to figure out that this thing is bigger than she's willing to admit. That being with me wouldn't be the hit to her career she's afraid it would. And if I had to guess, she's probably going to need some time to accept how serious I am— because what the media shows of me doesn't exactly scream quality boyfriend material. That shit is skewed, but I haven't done as much as I should have to set the record straight.

I will though, because for the first time in a long time, I've got a goal that really matters.

---

*Julia*

"CRIPES, Julia, how many times are you going to check your phone?"

I flip it facedown on the arm of the couch and give Cammy an apologetic smile. Matty's been in bed for an hour, and we're curled up on opposite couches for a movie night. My heart isn't really in it, but we planned this a week ago, and Cammy even got a bottle of wine out.

"I'm done," I promise.

She shakes her head and pauses whatever movie we've been watching.

Doesn't that say it all? I don't even know what's playing, except that I'm pretty sure it's a romantic comedy.

"*Just friends* Greg Baxter distracting you over there?"

"Don't get all worked up. His posts are funny is all."

"Mmhmm. I can tell. You've been snickering for the past twenty minutes."

I shake my head. "No, it was mostly the movie, I swear."

"Liar," Cammy gasps, her tone so *shame-on-you* I know I'm missing something.

Another glance at the TV and I gasp.

"*Cujo?*"

What. The. Hell?

"Now she notices." Cammy leans into the corner of her couch, cuddling her wine against her chest. "You're into him, sis. Admit it."

I can't. Because then I'd have to stop with the texts and calls, and I don't want to. I want the laughter and teasing and *friendly* flirtation I can still file under harmless. But if I'm *into* Greg, then all that changes.

Suddenly, he's not just the friend keeping a smile on my face. He turns into a guy with the potential to wipe it away for good.

Ray pulled me into his office again this week. He had a file on Greg, filled with pictures and printed articles. In each shot, he was standing with a different celebrity date, most of them known for drama, though none of it had been tied to him.

I've seen the pictures. Read the articles. Teased him about what a dirty player he is.

None of it bothered me until I was standing there with Ray too close as he flipped through the pages that were apparently circulating upstairs.

"I told them there's nothing to it," he'd said, rubbing my shoulders like he wanted to soothe me or something equally absurd. "That you were one hundred percent dedicated to your career, and even if you did decide to make room for a romantic entanglement, you would be too smart to invite this kind of tabloid fodder into your life. They're going to trust you, because *I* trust you, Julie. So for now, consider that fire put out."

I thanked him, stepping away before he could see how repulsed I was by having his hands on me, or how much I disliked him casting Greg in such a disparaging light.

But he'd made his point, and as much as I didn't like it, I couldn't ignore it.

I look back to Cammy, who's watching me expectantly. "We're goofing around. That's all. It's just how Greg is."

"So, same as always?"

I open my mouth and close it again.

"Fine, it's different. But the flirty stuff is only part of it. Half the time, all we're doing is texting back and forth about our days."

Eyes wide, she nods. "Like a couple."

"No." I'm standing my ground on this one.

It's been two weeks since Martin's party, and Greg hasn't asked me out again or hinted at wanting more than what we already have. What he has done is managed to integrate the subject of our sketchy hookups into our everyday conversations to the point where there's no weirdness around them at all. And while we used to go months between texts and sometimes years between calls, these days our limit is more like a few hours. It's like our little indiscretions have actually made us better friends.

The sound of my sister clearing her throat brings me back to *Cujo* and the smug smile perched on Cammy's lips.

"You should see the look on your face, Julia. You've got it bad."

I shake my head. "No, I've got it good. Greg's just the kind of friend I need in my life right now."

"The dirty kind?"

*Yes.* "No. The kind who makes me feel good."

"Girl, I don't disagree. This business with where

your career is going has been like a wet blanket over you for far too long. All I'm saying is, call this thing with Greg what it is."

Apparently, she's waiting for me to say it, because after an exasperated huff, she adds, "Which is *more than just friends*! Julia, how can we even be having this conversation?"

"Because I don't want anything more with Greg, okay?" I take a breath and meet my sister's eyes, wondering how, of all people, she doesn't understand. "I want things to stay the same, Cammy. I want him to be the friend I get to keep. The guy who doesn't have the chance to let me down. I want to be smart and make the choices that mean a stable, secure life for us. For Matty."

Cammy sits back, her eyes softening. "You're scared."

"I'm *cautious*."

"I guess between Mom and me demonstrating what a wrecking ball relationships can bring to your goals, it'd be hard to be anything else."

I hold up my hand, not wanting to put my issues on her, but she waves me off. "I get why you have a tough time letting guys in. I mean, aside from your dad and whoever mine is being two black holes in our lives, it's not exactly like Mom picked any winners."

Shaking my head, I let myself think back to the veritable revolving door of losers Mom brought home with her. The ones we knew were bad and avoided from the start. The ones who looked like they were better but ended up causing the most problems. And rarely, the ones we'd wished would stay, but never did. "How could anyone have such bad luck with men?"

I mean, I know so many good guys. Great guys. Couples with happy marriages. How could one woman so consistently pick duds?

Cammy shrugs. "She has a type?"

I look at my sister, sweet and beautiful and smart, and pregnant at seventeen with the baby of a boy who swore he'd love her forever, but the minute things got rough, bailed on her completely.

"I know you're thinking about Jeremy," she says, suddenly looking older, her eyes a little harder. "Wondering if I've got a type too. Or maybe if you do."

"No." It might be exactly what I'm worried about, but I'll never admit it to her.

She lets out short laugh and shakes her head. "Well, *I* think it doesn't matter what our types were in the past —yours, insufferably boring. Mine, somewhat unreliable. What matters is that we learn from our experiences and be open to giving the right man a chance when we find him. And if you're worried about history repeating itself with another guy who leaves, think about this… Greg's stuck around for thirteen years. Seriously, what else has the guy got to do to prove himself?"

I laugh, shocked to realize that he's been a man I've

trusted and relied on for nearly half of my life. In all that time he's never let me down.

But the leery voice in my head has to ask if maybe that's only because I've never given him the chance.

"There's more to it than trust, Cammy."

"I know. The job stuff. Your street cred and all that."

She's ridiculous, but I love her.

My watch vibrates, and I pinch my lips together, resisting the pull of the incoming text as Cammy watches me patiently. She reaches for her wine and takes a slow sip.

My fingers itch. My heart is already beating faster. I don't need to check it. I—

"You know what? I'm going to go check this. You watch *Cujo*. I'll keep you company later."

The corners of her mouth curl up, and she nods. "You do that."

I walk into my room, my phone pressed against my stomach until I close the door behind me. Sitting back on my bed, I check the message and grin.

**Greg: Time to chat with your favorite guy?**

I call him within a blink, and before the first ring is through, he answers.

"Jules, you should have seen it. Rux was signing autographs after our press thing, and this lady holding a squalling baby hands him a puck to sign. Rux is trying to be cool, but no one can hear anything over the wails. And then it's silence. Everyone stops and looks over to where the baby opens its mouth and goes Exorcist all over Rux. Green pea puke is literally dripping from his chin."

"Oh God. Is the baby okay?"

The answering laughter is rich and deep and rumbles through me in all the best ways.

"Baby was fine. Started doing that cute gurgling thing and playing with its toes."

I shouldn't like it that Greg thinks gurgly noises from babies are cute, but his hotness factor just went up by ten.

"And Rux, how was he?"

Another deep laugh. "Not so good. He's a sympathetic puker."

He goes on painting the picture of Rux trying to hold it together in front of the fans and failing in spectacular fashion, and by the time he's done, I'm laughing so hard tears are spilling down my cheeks.

When I take a breath, Greg sighs. "Damn, you've got the best laugh."

"Yours isn't so bad either. I like hearing it."

"Yeah, well I'll be home in a couple of days and maybe we can do some laughing in person."

I can see us hanging out. Grabbing a bite or a beer. Watching *The Walking Dead* on his couch. I can see talking to him like this, while I lie back on my bed… only with him beside me.

It's crazy. I shouldn't be thinking that way at all. But maybe Cammy's right.

My phone starts to vibrate with an incoming message. Then another and another.

"Hold on a second, Greg. My phone is blowing up."

"Everything okay?"

I check the incoming texts and shoot upright, a cough punching free from my lungs.

Oh God, this is bad.

"Jules?"

Staring at the image the network PR manager attached, I take a slow breath.

"What's going on?" he asks, his tone urgent.

"Someone took a few pictures of me at the gym today. I wasn't doing anything wrong, but they look— my boss isn't going to like this."

## Chapter 9

*Greg*

TWO DAYS AGO, I was pretty fucking happy about the way things were shaping up with Julia. We'd been talking, texting, getting closer with every conversation. I could hear her defenses coming down with each soft sigh and lingering goodbye. And up until this thing with the gym photos, I was thinking all I needed was to get back in town, and that chemical thing between us that reacts every time my mouth gets close to hers would do the rest.

Now I'm not so sure.

I hadn't fully appreciated exactly how big an obstacle Julia's job actually is. Doesn't matter that there's nothing specific in her contract about athletes outside the NFL. The problem is the uphill battle she's fighting for credibility in a field predominantly ruled by dudes.

I'm no stranger to protecting my public image. There are clauses in my contracts about conduct too. But for Julia, it's more than avoiding scandal or bad behavior that could keep her off a Wheaties box. It's everything from how loose her sweater fits to whether her smile lasted a second too long. Finding that fractional space between coming across as a cold bitch and coming across like she's coming on to someone.

There's always a camera and always someone looking to judge her on all the shit that's no one's fucking business but hers.

The photos are stupid.

Julia was working out, wearing the same tight tank and fitted shorts everyone else wears—granted, that combo looks a hell of a lot better on her than on most people—but some dickcheese snapped a few shots of her when one of the NBA guys happened to be at the club too. The whole interaction took less than ten seconds and was limited to him saying hi and her complimenting his winning shot in the game from a few nights before, but the guy looks like he's staring at her tits, and she looks like she's giving him the pie eye. This shit happens all the time, but it doesn't always result in a viral meme. Julia's did.

As a result, I'm not going to get to see her before she leaves for her next game.

"I'm sorry, Greg. The meeting was a total waste of

time. At least it wasn't with wardrobe again—I don't think I could have taken another debate over the thickness of my sweater for the next game."

She lets out a laugh, but it's cold and tired and not the one I love to hear.

"This'll blow over, Jules. There's nothing to it."

She's quiet for a moment, and I want to put my arms around her. I want to kiss her hair and feel her melt into me. Be the comfort I know she needs.

But we aren't there yet, and this bullshit isn't getting us any closer, that's for sure.

"It's the *perception*. It's—"

"It's bullshit, but it's part of the job you have." I get it.

"Yeah."

Last night she was throwing the F-word around again. *Friends.* I don't like it, but with the shit she's putting up with at work, all I want is to make things easier for her, not harder.

So we can play at *just* friends a little longer, but sooner or later it's not going to be enough for either of us. That's when we'll bury the *just* between us, once and for all.

I rub a hand over my chest. Damn, I can't wait.

But for now... "You get the Xbox game I sent you?"

She laughs, and it's soft and warm and only for me. "I did. Soccer's an interesting pick."

I settle deeper against the headboards. "Figured neither one of us would have an unfair advantage. But you can only practice at it for one hour before we play online."

"Worried I'm gonna shame you?"

Absolutely.

We talk some more, the conversation lightening as we skip around from Matty's preschool crush to Rux's new car to the salad Julia ate for dinner. When she gives in to her first yawn, I offer to drive over and tuck her in. And I get the laugh I was hoping for.

A few more days and I'll get a yes.


"WAIT—'NO'?" I shake my head and plant one fist on the kitchen counter as Julia spins into yet another excuse as to why we can't meet up in person. Again.

It's been another two weeks, and while our travel schedules haven't exactly lined up, there have been opportunities. And now this.

"I mean, that sneeze. He could be coming down with a bug. Kids pick up everything, you know? I couldn't live with myself if you got sick because of me. Especially in the middle of the season."

Her words are rushed, almost pleading. A part of me wants to laugh at what a shit liar she is, because it's kind of adorable—but the greater part of me is pissed. This isn't about Matty having a bug. Just like three days ago wasn't about Cammy needing a girls' night in.

Cammy's got Instagram too. I follow her, and the

posts from that night were all about being bored out of her mind and wishing she hadn't cancelled her plans.

Julia's still talking about the various strains of flu going around when I cut her off.

"You're dodging me. At least, dodging *seeing* me." We're talking more than ever, so I know it's not like she isn't interested. "What gives?"

Silence.

"Look, Greg, I want to see you. I do. But I'm… nervous."

Now we're getting somewhere. "Nervous about what?"

"Things have been so good with us. Maybe I'm a little nervous about rocking the boat. I like what we have. And I don't want to mess it up."

"Mess it up how?"

She sighs, and I imagine her biting her plush bottom lip, and those heavy-lidded eyes cutting away from me.

"No one crosses any lines when it's just us talking. I mean, no one crosses any *real* lines. It's not only the stuff going on with work. The perception stuff. It's what might actually happen between us. I mean, we flirt and tease, and innuendo is practically your second language. But when it's over the phone, it's safe."

"You're worried I'll cross the line if we see each other?"

That laugh. Damn.

"I'm worried you'll cross all of them."

She's a smart woman, but this time she's wrong. "Julia, give it a chance. I swear, I'll let you set the tone. Trust me?"

If anyone's going to cross the line, it's her.

———

*Julia*

"You sound like you're putting makeup on."

I blink at my reflection in the compact I'm holding. "What? Greg, seriously, how did you know that?" I spin around in my seat, checking out the windows to see if maybe he's in the car beside me—but no.

His chuckle is low. "Your words get a little slower, softer around the edges."

There's a thrill of satisfaction in knowing he's listening so carefully.

"You nervous?"

He isn't asking about the charity dinner I'll be speaking at this evening, and I know it. He's asking about seeing him.

About the two of us sharing space in the same room for the first time since the incident at Martin's party.

"Are you?"

"Nah. Excited to see you. Want to get my hug on and see that sweet smile in person."

"Yeah, I know how you feel." I want to leave it at

that, but I can't. "But, um, Greg. This is us being friends. I mean, really, just friends." I sigh, watching as we cut through the downtown traffic. "I feel bad even saying it, but you promised."

"Don't feel bad. And don't worry. As insanely hot as what happened last time was, I'm not about to push for something you don't want. I swore you'll be the one who sets the tone, and I'll follow. Promise."

I relax into the deep backseat.

Then there's nothing to worry about.

I arrive at the benefit early to meet with Georgina and Stuart. I've been to too many of these things to count, but even I'm taken aback by the elegance of the grand ballroom. Georgina waves to me from across the vast room, signaling toward Stuart, who's already heading my way.

"Julia!" He greets me with bright eyes and an affectionate kiss. "Georgina has been telling everyone about Mr. Baxter's attendance tonight. However you got him to agree, we're in your debt."

My smile is camera-ready as I answer. "We went to high school together and I saw him at our reunion last month. The timing happened to work."

"Is he with you?"

"No. But I'm sure he'll arrive soon."

Stuart introduces me to a few of the key players for the benefit and shows me where I'll need to stand and when to be ready. Soon the room begins to fill.

It's a great turnout, and from all accounts, donations are expected to surpass our goal.

I'm talking with an older couple from Lake Forest when I happen to glance up, and whatever I was in the middle of saying dries on my tongue, the breath leaks from my lungs, and everything… stops.

*Greg.* He steps out of the elevator, wearing that brazenly confident, criminally sexy smile slanted across his mouth, looking completely devastating in the custom tux he warned me about last week. My heart starts to pound as he nods to someone passing by and shoots his cuffs, laughing at a joke I'm too far away to hear.

I can't take my eyes off him. Not just because of the immaculate cut of his tux or seeing his perpetually wild hair smoothed back into a style so neat my fingers itch with the need to delve into it. But because this is the first time I've laid eyes on him since Martin's party, and the impact of actually seeing him in person after a month and a half—as opposed to watching the footage from his games or having this larger-than-life man safely reduced to the rectangle on my phone—is overwhelming me in a way I should have expected… but didn't.

God, he's tall.

*This is bad.*

And broad.

*Very bad.*

He's barely arrived, and already I feel the crazy pull

that has nothing to do with thirteen years of friendship and everything to do with those scant few minutes we threw caution to the wind.

I'm stronger than this.

I know better.

I can't believe how good his legs look when he walks.

Swallowing, I drag my eyes up but get stuck on the single button closing his jacket. His stomach is hard-packed perfection beneath that jacket. His chest too. And his shoulders. God, I shouldn't be thinking about the rounded balls of his shoulders. I shouldn't be mentally peeling him out of that tux or calling up the memories of those precious few moments when I got to touch him. I shouldn't be staring at him at all.

My eyes creep higher. Up the thick column of his neck, over the clean-shaven lines of his solid jaw to his mouth. His dirty, dirty mouth.

My own mouth gets dry as I think about the gruff sound of his voice and the things he's already said to me.

I follow the broken line of his masculine nose to his hard blue eyes… staring straight back at me.

Uh-oh.

## Chapter 10

*Greg*

*I*'M NOT EVEN all the way into the ballroom when I see her. Julia's surrounded by couples decked out in their most elegant attire, but she blows them all away. She's fucking gorgeous. She's wearing a sheer dress in deep red that breaks a few inches above her knees and drapes close enough to her curves to hint at them without giving away exactly what's there. It's sexy and bold, while somehow keeping her modest at the same time. Her hair is pinned up in a not-too-neat twist that shows off the bare length of her neck… and she's watching me. And not in an *ooh look, my favorite pal just showed up* way either.

Pals don't catch their breath when they see you. They don't let their eyes do that slow-crawl thing down your body and then, even slower, back up again. And they definitely don't turn that particular shade of scarlet when they realize you've seen the whole thing and then turn away like maybe the singe marks on your tux will go away if they pretend it didn't happen.

Not a chance, Jules.

She set the tone with that look, and I'm ready to follow. As in, I'm checking the exits, wondering whether the clasp on her dress is on the back or the side, and starting to speculate about what her lip gloss tastes like. Fine, I was thinking about that before I even left my building, but honestly, I thought I'd have longer to wait before Julia flat-out broke every rule she'd made with one single scorching look.

I don't make it more than two feet when a woman dressed in some kind of black tent with rhinestones the size of my thumb around the neck stops in front of me, introducing herself as Georgina, the coordinator for the event.

She's attractive, probably around fifty, and before I can take another step toward the ballroom or Julia within it, this little bulldozer hustles me toward a private room off to the side.

"Some of our biggest contributors are hockey fans, so we thought you might have a drink alone with them before the rest of the evening kicks off."

I want to go find Julia before she can talk herself into believing that look was anything other than what it was. The deathblow to the *just* she keeps propping up between us.

But that's not why we're here. Or not the only reason, anyway.

I follow Georgina, and when I step into the Astor Room, I'm met with cheers. The guys surrounding me are dressed in custom tuxes on par with mine, but with studs and links that probably cost more than my first car. They walk over, offering handshakes and congratulations on our last win and the season in general.

It's flattering, and if every molecule in my being wasn't focused on getting back to Julia and finding out how she intends to go forward from here, I'd be all about shooting the shit for awhile. As it is, I force myself to engage.

Nod.

Smile.

Thank you.

Repeat.

My phone vibrates in my pocket, signaling a text. It could be Nat asking to score some tickets for her friends… or it could be Julia, trying to talk me out of what I just saw.

I want it to be Julia, so I can tell her where to meet me, so we can put this charade behind us once and for all. Her career can handle a relationship. Even one with an athlete.

But pulling out my phone to check a text would be shitty. I don't want to be that guy. So I give the contributors the time they bid on, talk up the charity we're all supporting in the hopes that by the time they walk out tonight, they feel good enough to cut another check.

It's not too long before Georgina is back. The guys clap me on the shoulder and shake my hand, thanking me for coming out and wishing me and the team luck through the rest of the season.

"Greg, I've got a few friends I'd love for you to meet." Georgina the bulldozer hooks her arm through mine, no doubt ready to lead me around for the rest of the night. It's the reason I'm here, at least on paper. But I need a minute.

"Actually, I've got a call I need to make. Mind if I hang back? I'll find you when I'm through."

I flash a smile and then wait for her to leave before walking over to the windows overlooking the river and pulling out my phone. There's a single message from Julia.

**Julia: It was an accident.**

An accident. Like maybe if she'd realized I was walking in, she would have braced herself? The way *just* friends shouldn't have to.

I'm already dialing.

"Greg," she says. I can hear the apology in her voice alongside the din of the party. "I think you're going to have to tease me or something, so I know we're okay."

"Tease you about what? The way you stripped me naked and did dirty things to me with your eyes?"

"Yeah, that." She pauses. "Where are you?"

"Astor Room. Left of the elevators. But I'm about to go make the rounds with Georgina."

"Right. Well, I'll see you later then."

"Julia?"

"Yes?"

"When you do… we're going to talk about that look."

---

*Julia*

I DON'T WANT to talk about that look. In fact, up until ten seconds ago, I'd been doing a bang-up job of ensuring we haven't had the opportunity to discuss it all evening. It's a big ballroom, and if Greg happened to be at the north end, I managed to stay south. The few times I couldn't stop our paths from crossing, I made sure to pull someone, anyone, along with me, thus ensuring the conversation stayed far, far away from *the look* that got away from me.

Until now, it had been working. Unfortunately, my conversation buffer saw her fiancé come in, and now the little traitor has sprinted off, leaving me staring up at Greg. Nothing to distract me from this gorgeous man in his tuxedo and the trouble I'm having keeping my eyes to myself.

I'm surrounded by good-looking men on a regular basis, and it never gets to me. But with Greg, I can barely breathe. I can hardly look at him without heat spilling into my cheeks, and as to tearing my eyes away? Forget it.

Which is crazy. I'm not fifteen. This isn't my first crush.

It's not a crush at all.

It's Greg, one of my oldest friends and the guy I promised I wouldn't objectify tonight. We're friends. Just friends.

With no more hookups between us.

No more kissing.

No more flirting.

I shake my head, mentally amending the no-more-flirting clause, because *this is Greg*. Flirting is like breathing for him—an involuntary response, and one I sort of cherish.

But no more staring!

"Thought we discussed you avoiding me," he says.

Don't look at him. Don't look at him. Don't—

God, he's so handsome it hurts.

A waiter passes by, and I swipe a glass of white wine from his tray. "I'm not."

He lets out a low laugh that slides right through to the deepest parts of me.

"Glad to hear it." He steps closer, ducking his head so his next words are directed at me and me alone. We're standing in the middle of hundreds of people, but when his eyes are on me like that, a glint of amusement edging a more serious intent, it feels like we're alone. "Should we discuss that look?"

My cheeks burn hotter, and I toss back half my glass in one swallow. "It was just one look."

I'm such a liar.

He laughs again, letting up on the eye contact as he surveys the crowd. "There's that *just* word again. I'm starting to think maybe you don't think it means what it really means. And P.S. … it wasn't just one."

Geeze. This guy. "Greg, we're past it. Everything is fine."

So long as I don't look at any part of him for more than a fraction of a second, we're totally good.

"You sure?"

No. But I'm subscribing to the fake-it-'til-you-make-it school of thought here. "Absolutely."

He rolls his shoulder in my peripheral vision. "Well, that's a relief."

"Good." It's definitely good. Right? I hazard another look at his face. "But out of curiosity, can I ask why?"

The corner of his mouth curves, and I feel the tug of it all the way through me.

"Because if you *weren't* past it—if, for example, another one of those rogue looks got away from you while we were in the midst of this crowd—I could see where that might be a problem."

I force myself to focus on the orchestra set up across the room. Only Greg isn't done.

"But even if by some miracle *they* don't catch the look in your eyes, and *I* do… then we'd have to worry about *them* seeing the look in *mine*. The one that says it's only going to be a matter of seconds before I've got one hand in your hair and the other finding out what's under that incredible dress."

I try to swallow, but my throat makes a dry clicking sound, so I drain my glass.

Taking the empty from my hand, Greg returns it to a passing waiter.

He's amused, the sexy jerk. He knew exactly what kind of effect that casual reference to getting under my dress would have.

"Good thing there's zero chance of another one of those looks getting away from me. Ever."

Okay, *ever* is probably a stretch, but he doesn't have to snort about it. Cocky bastard.

I should let it go. Let him have his little laugh.

Taking the drink from his hand, I tap my index finger against the condensation-covered glass before bringing it to my lips. Club soda and lime.

It's not strong enough to justify what blurts past my lips, but I can't stop myself. "So you don't need to give what kind of *tiny* and *delicate* I've got going on under this dress another thought."

His body stiffens, and his eyes cut to my chest. He's built like a superhero, but despite his apparent laser focus, I'm pretty sure he doesn't actually have X-ray vision.

All I wanted was the satisfaction of seeing him squirm. Maybe to gloat a little.

But neither one of us is the type to relinquish a win so easily.

"Jules, you're going to have to be careful. Tiny and delicate sounds like it might not survive these *rough* hands of mine."

My breath catches as need spears through me, and my center goes hot and liquid.

I open my mouth, wanting to say something sharp that puts him in his place. But I can't make a sound. I can't think about anything but the snap of elastic and my panties falling apart in his big… rough… hands.

Greg seems to be waiting for the comeback that isn't coming too.

The seconds stretch and pull.

Our eyes meet and, suddenly, that smug satisfaction washes clean off his face as his nostrils flare and his eyes turn to midnight. I'm pretty sure this is the look he warned me about.

"Aww, fuck. Now you've done it, Jules."

I take a shaky breath. "I know."

# Chapter 11

*M*Y SHOULDERS HIT the Goethe Room's back wall, followed less than a blink later by Greg's chest meeting mine in a hard, full-body press. He's kissing me like a man possessed. His mouth hot and demanding, his tongue pushing past my lips, filling me with an erotic thrust that has my hips chasing his.

I'm shaking, I want this so bad. Need it.

This is reckless. Crazy. But I can't stop. I don't want to stop.

Greg has an uncanny knack for locating unused and out-of-the-way spaces. No one's seen us together. No one knows what we're doing.

So what's one more time?

My fingers trace his heavy jaw. Though he was clean-shaven when he arrived, I can already feel the hint of stubble. But it's not the rough touch I'm after.

"More," I say, between kisses so wet and hot and dirty I wonder if I could come from them alone.

His teeth close around my bottom lip, biting gently into the soft flesh as he gives it a tug, setting off a series of flutters deep inside me.

I need more. More than Greg kissing me.

My arms close around his neck, pulling us into closer contact, but still not close enough.

"My dress," I gasp, desperate to get my legs around him.

"You want me to touch you?" he growls against my ear, sliding his big hand up my thigh to bring the sheer layers and slip with it. "You want my fingers inside you, Jules?"

He's between my legs, skimming the edge of my panties. Reminding me of his promise from earlier.

Heat pools at my center, and my belly churns with frantic need.

"*Greg.*"

He hooks a finger in the side and twists enough so there's no mistaking his intent. "This?"

I'm so focused on the tension at my waist I can barely think.

"*Yes,*" I whisper, trembling beneath his touch.

A low groan rumbles from deep in his chest, and

then I have what I'm asking for, the bite of my lingerie giving way at one hip and then the other. The damp scrap of my panties being drawn from my sensitive folds, followed by the kiss of cool air.

This is reckless, crazy. But I can't stop.

The blunt end of his finger runs the length of my sex in a tease that leaves me breathless. Clinging to his shoulders as I wait for what he'll give me next.

His lips are at my ear, brushing up and down against the lobe. "I'm not going to fuck you, Jules," he growls, his breath tickling my skin in a way that has me purring, arching into his—

"Wait—what?"

His laughter is a low rumble I feel *everywhere*.

"I can't stop thinking about you. About the little sounds you make when I touch you… like this." His finger presses in, sinking deep, deeper, all the way inside.

*Just like that.*

I rock into him, restless for more.

"So fucking wet," he says. "You're killing me."

"Please," I gasp, then again, louder when he slides out before sinking back in. It's so hot, so good.

"You feel so nice. I'm going to kiss you, and I'm going to touch you, because I've been going out of my mind for weeks. But that's it. Five minutes, Jules…" He adds another finger, working them both deep inside me. It almost feels like too much, like more than I can take, and yet not enough. "Five minutes, and then we're going back out there." His fingers flex and spread as he twists them inside me. "You're going to say goodbye at one end of the room. I'm going to say goodbye at the other. Then I'm going to put you in my car and take you home, and when we get there, I'm going to fuck you so hard you'll feel me for days. But not here. Not like this." He pulls back, and that slick, probing touch comes to a stop. "Not until you admit we're *together*."

I gasp, my heart pounding as his gorgeous blue eyes hold mine. "Greg."

"Together, Jules. No *just* about it. Not just this once. Not just one more time. Not just friends. Together. You and me."

My fingers drift from his hair, splaying wide over his chest. This is where I tell him I can't, that I don't want what he's offering. My career is too important. I have rules.

Only I can't lie to myself anymore. I can't lie to either of us.

I've never wanted anyone the way I want him.

My career shouldn't have anything to do with what happens between Greg and me.

And those rules? I've been breaking them since day one with him. I was just too scared to admit it.

*I trust him.*

I brush my thumb across his lower lip. "There's one *just* I can't let go of."

Eyes narrowed, he asks, "What's that?"

*"This is just between us."*

A slow grin spreads across his gorgeous face, and he pulls me tight for another claiming kiss. When he breaks away it's to mutter, "Five minutes."

I start playing with the studs on his shirt. "Before we have to go back out?"

It's not a lot of time, but I'm thinking it's enough to get up to some serious no good.

He shakes his head. "Five minutes to say goodbye and get your sweet ass into my car. We've waited long enough."

———

*Greg*

EVEN WITH HER trembling in my arms and those soft brown eyes peering up at me with undisguised need, I'm not sure she'll agree. But when she does? Damn, it takes everything I have to let her go.

Especially with the remains of those hot-as-fuck panties burning a hole in my pocket.

Julia's a pro and manages to pull herself together in less than thirty seconds. Me… well, the man downstairs has some other ideas, and talking him into waiting to act on them takes a few minutes. By the time I return to the party, looking more or less the way I did when I left it, Julia is through with her goodbyes.

One last glance over the smooth line of her shoulder, and she steps into the elevator to leave.

I've already talked to my driver, who picks her up in front of the hotel and then circles around to the loading dock and waits for me.

There's no press. No one from the benefit. And of the couple guys who noticed me cutting out the back way, the only thing they have to say is, "Good game last night, Baxter."

I don't wait for the driver to get the door, folding myself into the dimly lit backseat as fast as it takes to line up a shot. The privacy shield is already up. Julia is perched at the edge of her seat. She looks as nervous as I've ever seen her. Things are changing between us, and hell, I get it. It's a big deal. But like I told her, we're together now. I cross to her side of the car and pull her across my lap.

It's exactly the right thing to do, because she goes from tense to lax within the span of a shocked squeak, melting into my chest, peering up at me with those soft eyes.

"Are we really doing this?"

I run my hand along the outside of her hip and thigh, enjoying the way she seems to snuggle into the contact. "You better believe we are."

She bites her bottom lip. "Greg, we've been friends for so long. If what we're doing doesn't work out—I don't want to lose you."

Bowing my head, I press a kiss to the lip she just

abused and suck it gently into my mouth to lick at the swell. I feel the catch of her breath quake through her body. "You won't. I promise, Julia. We'll always be friends first." It's why I feel so good about what we're doing. We have something I've never had with someone else… trust. Thirteen years of it. Julia has no idea how big of a deal that is for me, but it is.

Her fingers slip into my hair, bringing me back for another hungry kiss. "I need you," she whispers, and I'm not sure if either one of us could say whether she means in this moment or in her life. I like to think both. It's how *I* feel. We've always been in sync. "Greg, I haven't been able to stop thinking about you. I tried."

"I know, Jules." Our kisses are escalating, like now that we've given in, there's nothing holding them back. She purrs, and that sound has me nearly out of my mind. I pull her tighter against my chest, the shift enough for her to crawl across my lap. Her skirt bunches in my hands around her hips, her knees straddling my thighs as she moans around the thrust of my tongue.

I knead her ass with one hand while I slide the other between her legs. She's wet and warm and open to me, her panties little more than a keepsake in my pocket. Petting through her lush folds is going to be the end of me. Her eyes haze, her lips parted as she hovers over me, the spread of her sex mine for the taking.

I want in.

I want to tear my fucking fly open and slam up

inside her ready, wet heat. I want to feel her come around me, her snug little pussy clenching and sucking at my cock the way it did around my fingers.

I told her I wasn't going to fuck her back at the benefit, and no matter how much I want to, I'm not going to fuck her in this limo either. I made sure of that when I emptied the condoms from my wallet before I left the house.

It's torture knowing I have to wait, but it's the kind of torture I'm not above making the most of.

"Did you like your present?" I murmur against her ear between wet kisses and almost-gentle bites. I'm talking about the vibrator I sent her after the last time she *just friended* me.

I have to know. "Did you use it?"

She moans, her knees gripping my hips.

"Is that a yes, Julia?" I ask, even though I know, fuck yeah, it is. And now I'm seeing that pink orb in my mind, imagining the way it would vibrate between her fingers.

Another full-body tremor, and her fists tighten in my shirt. "*Yes.*"

So hot, and because she gave me what I wanted, I give her a little more in return. Her clit is swollen, throbbing beneath my finger as I circle it a few slow times. "Did it make you come?"

*Did I make you come?*

She shudders, and I kiss her hard, giving her my

tongue in deep, claiming thrusts. She moans around me and something wild races in my chest.

I tug at her earlobe with my teeth. "Did you put it inside you?"

"*Greg*." She rocks into my hand in a needy plea that might actually kill me.

"We're *friends*," I murmur, brushing my lips against her delicate ear a few times, because feeling her unraveling in my arms is a rush right up there with winning the Stanley Cup. "You can tell me."

"Yes," she gasps, rocking harder. "*Yes*."

A low groan rumbles free from my throat. "So jealous, Jules." It's nuts, but true. I am.

Following her slick seam, I tease her opening before dipping a finger inside. "Was it as good as this?"

The catch of her breath is more satisfying than the last six times I got off… combined.

I give her a second finger, savoring the clasp and hug that comes with every inch I penetrate. She's soaked, her need coating my fingers, driving me fucking insane.

"So wet, Jules. Did you get this wet using my toy?"

"God, Greg. You feel—I can't—"

I'm pretty sure she can. Especially when her hips lift to my touch. All the better to access the sweetest spot I've ever been. My dick's ready to bust through my fly, but until we get back to my building, this is all I can give her.

"Yeah, you can. I'm going to make you come all over my hand, Julia."

Every time I open my mouth, that hug gets stronger. My girl likes a little dirty talk. The heel of my hand meets the spread of her sex and I ask, "Was it a tight fit, Jules?"

She gasps, clenching around me again.

"Did you have to work to get it inside you?"

"Y-yes."

I know she did. I saw the dimensions when I ordered it and I'm betting it was a little smaller than the fingers I'm giving her now.

My hands are huge.

"It gets me so fucking hard to imagine you using it. Sliding it around your clit and then taking it deep."

She lets out a kitten-soft cry, rocking into each slow, probing thrust.

"What were you thinking about when you pushed it inside?" It's a risk to ask. I mean, if she tells me Ryan Gosling, it's really going to blow the mood. Although I know myself well enough to admit a challenge like that wouldn't end too badly for her. I wouldn't be able to let her walk away until I was sure I'd obliterated any fantasy about anyone else she'd ever had.

"*Mmm*, I was thinking about *you*."

Fuck. I don't expect her breathless admission to hit me like it does, but it shakes me up, moves things around deep in my chest so that she's there, a part of me.

The car comes to a stop, and we both look out the tinted windows to the private garage beyond. With the exception of a few high-end vehicles, it's empty.

"This is your building?" she whispers, fumbling off my lap.

"Yeah." I check that she's got her dress in place and then open the door and help her out. "No one is going to see you. When Hank Wagner lived here, he helped Jack upgrade the security. It's completely private, so you don't need to worry about anyone grabbing a picture of you." I'm walking toward the residents' elevator, towing her behind as quickly as she can keep up in her heels. We need to get inside and finish what we started all those weeks ago beneath the bleachers. I'm mentally counting the steps it should take to get from the elevator to my bed. Calculating in zippers and buttons and links.

We ride up with her hand in mine, silence surrounding us, the air thick with tension. I want my mouth back on her and the needy clutch of her fingers in my hair. But until we're in my apartment, there's security, and no way am I letting Erwin or Gabe get a look at what's only for me.

The elevator opens on my floor, and I let us into my apartment. The door closes behind us, and it's on.

Our mouths are fused as we yank and pull at our clothes. I'm pretty sure I hear a seam pop in my haste to get free of this monkey suit. Jules, though, I have naked in a flash. The sheer and silky layers of her dress dangle from the entry table, and thanks to our antics at the party, her panties have already been handled. Which leaves her in a pair of shimmery heels and a pair of delicate gold drop earrings and not one damn thing more.

I'm on my knees in my tuxedo pants, no shirt, my mouth open against the soft curve of her ass, my hands sliding up to palm her full breasts and tease her nipples. I've been so careful not to leave a mark on her neck, but here…

"Greg," she gasps, reaching out to steady herself against the wall as I swirl my tongue over her toned cheek and suck hard enough to draw a splotch of purple to her flawless skin.

*Mine.*

"Turn around."

"So bossy." Her laugh is breathless, beautiful, and has more power over me than anyone or anything should. She does as I ask. "Like this?"

Almost. After a lengthy caress, I guide one flawless leg over my shoulder and look up to meet her eyes. "Like *this*."

Yeah, she knows exactly what comes next.

Her fingers sift into my hair. Fucking heaven.

Without breaking eye contact, I kiss her. Soft and light. A kiss here. A kiss there. Her thigh. Her slick folds.

Deeper.

Longer.

With tongue.

I've dreamt of this, only having my mouth on her is even better than those pent-up fantasies.

The tug of her fingers intensifies. "*So good, Greg.*"

I lick through her sweetness, dipping inside and circling her clit with the tip of my tongue. Rubbing with the flat of it.

She's got my hair in a death grip that has me never wanting to cut it again. Soft cries and broken pleas rain down on me. I want to drown in them. I want my name on her lips when I make her come like this, and I want it to be the best she's ever had.

Because that's what it is for me. I haven't even gotten inside her yet, but knowing this is the start of something real with Julia—*fuck.*

There's nothing hotter than when she starts to rock into my mouth, her body begging for more. I can feel her pulse and throb against my tongue, can taste how close she is.

I suck hard and she screams, coming apart while I hold her to my mouth. She's barely done when I scoop her up in my arms and carry her back to my room.

Jesus. Julia Wesley is *in my bed,* her chest is flushed, eyes hazed, and yeah, there might be a hickey on her inner thigh. Not gonna lie, it's getting me hard as fuck.

My pants are off, the condom on, and Julia's beneath me, her legs moving in a restless shift.

Then I'm there. The head of my cock pressing into the tight channel of her body. Our eyes meet. This is different than any of the lines we've crossed before. "We're together, Julia."

She nods, her hands framing my face. And even in the midst of this hot need, there's a hint of a smile on her lips when she whispers, "No *justs* about it."

I sink home.

## Chapter 12

*Greg*

I'VE WOKEN UP with plenty of women before, but waking up with Julia in my arms is like nothing else. She's sexy and vulnerable and trusting, and all I want is to wrap my arms tighter around her, hold her closer than I already am. Thing is, she's still sleeping, and as much as I want to get my squeeze on, I don't want to ruin what is, quite possibly, one of the most perfect moments I've ever had.

She smells fucking amazing, and I'm thinking about my bed smelling like her after she leaves and wondering if it would be weird to ask my housekeeper to skip a week washing the sheets.

There's a subtle change in her breathing, followed by the languid stretch of her body.

Taking my opportunity, I draw her closer, pressing my nose into her golden hair.

"Morning," she purrs, cuddling into my heat with a contented sound that has my inner caveman thumping his chest.

*Mine.*

"Morning, Jules. Sleep okay?"

"So good." It sounds like porn the way she says it, her morning voice all low and sultry. The sound of it goes straight to the man downstairs, and I feel like I've got to apologize for the way he's shoving at her hip.

She shifts again, turning on her side so she's facing me. Her bare breasts cushion against my chest, and her knee begins this leisurely up-and-down slide against my thigh. But it's those sleepy soft brown eyes peering up at me that get me the most. I'm so lost in them, I almost don't notice when her heel hooks around the back of my leg to draw me closer to the warm, wet—

Damn. I'm right there.

Right.

There.

If I thought I'd found heaven before, it had nothing on this.

"I was dreaming about you all night," she murmurs against my chest between butterfly kisses.

I reach for her hip, pulling her closer. It feels so good, so slick and warm and inviting, but all I'm willing to give either of us is the slow rock of my hips against that soft, needy place. I cradle the sweet curve of her ass in my hand, using it to move us together in a tease that's mostly torture. I'm not sure how long I'll be able to hold out.

"What were you dreaming about?" I want every detail.

"About this." She sighs as I slide through her slickness without sinking inside. "About the way you kiss me and hold me and what it's like when I have you inside me."

I rock again, and her breath catches, her eyes hazing over.

"What's it like?"

"Overwhelming. But in the best way." Another fractured breath as I tease the head of my cock over her clit. "It's like everything is too much when you're inside me. Like I'm not sure I can even handle it, but then I realize I don't have to. The only thing I need to do is give myself over, let go, and just feel you, filling me more than I ever thought I could be. Loving it."

She doesn't have any idea what her words are doing to me. She can't.

I want her in ways I've never wanted other women. I want *everything*.

I'm coated in her slickness, driving us both to the brink of madness with this skin-on-skin contact I would never give in to with someone else. But with Julia, I can't stop, I don't want to stop, until I've made her come. It's as close as I can get to what I really want.

Sinking inside her with nothing between us. No barriers.

The thought alone has me ready to spill with a deep guttural sound rumbling out of my chest as I push Julia back and knee her legs wide beneath me.

"Getting on top of you drives me fucking wild."

Her lips part on the kind of satisfying gasp that makes a guy think he can do anything.

I slide over that sweet spot again and feel the buck of her hips. The tightening of her fingers in my hair.

"Condom?" she asks breathlessly. Despite my rock-hard fantasy, I know I should get one. I know I've already taken this too far. That every time I give in and the blunt head of my cock grazes over her opening, pressing in just enough to drive us both crazy, I'm tempting fate in a way I never usually do.

Five seconds, hell, three, and I'll be suited up and sinking deep.

But that dark voice in my head keeps saying, *a few more seconds. A bit longer. A little deeper.*

"I want to feel you come like this. Then I'll get one." My hips haven't stopped moving. I'm propped on one elbow next to her head, cradling her ass to bring her hips up, sliding back and forth with my cock trapped between our bodies so the hard ridge of the head drags over her clit in a firm press. "I want my cock drenched in your come. I want to be dripping with it."

She's already soaked, and every word I say seems to be getting me closer to my end goal.

"Greg, mmm, please, oh God, so good. Like that, don't stop."

"You like this, Jules?" I know she does. I can feel her spasm even from the outside.

"I do." She's tensed, her breath coming in ragged bursts as her hips snap against mine. "I *love* it."

Jesus, I know she's talking about the sex. Fine, about my dick in particular, but hearing that forbidden L-word spill from her lips in conjunction with any part of me feels like getting called up for the draft.

"You're going to come for me."

"Yes, mmm, Greg. Right *there*."

I slow my movements and shorten my stroke, focusing on her needy little bud.

"Here?"

Her lips part on a stunted breath, her eyes going wide as they lock with mine. And I've got it. Exactly what I wanted… Julia coming against the bare skin of my cock, coating me with her pleasure.

I thought it would be enough, to have her this way. It's more unprotected contact than I've ever had. But fuck, I want more. Julia's eyes meet mine, and I can see what she's offering without words. We can do this. She'd let me into her perfect body… bare. Nothing between us.

That trust. It does something to me. It *means* something to me.

Emotion pushes at my chest. The way she's looking at me, I don't trust myself not to say something it's too soon to say. Instead I kiss her, sinking into the softest, slowest, most tender and heartfelt kiss I can give, tasting her lips with the barest lick of my tongue, and when she opens beneath me, sinking into her mouth and tasting her there.

So sweet.

Sweeter still when she moans around my next measured thrust.

I make love to her mouth, thoroughly, completely.

Dragging myself from the brink, I roll on some latex before I do something neither of us can take back.

Leaning over her, I find that soft point of give between her legs and, eyes locked with hers, sink home. The snug fit of her body taking mine is so hot, so good. I don't want to think about what it would have been like with nothing between us. How much louder her moans and cries would be. How hard I could make her come.

How she'd be the only one.

I want that.

For the first time since Shelly—shit. Don't go there. Not now. Not with Julia beneath me, around me.

This is enough. More than. I don't need to skip the rubber to make Julia lose her mind. I withdraw and, shifting my angle, push deep again. Her eyes go wide, and her breath escapes in a gasp. Deeper still, I rotate my hips, making sure she feels me everywhere.

I give her long and slow, hard and fast. Dirty and dirtier. Every trick in my book. Things I've only heard as rumor. All of it.

When I've made her come three times, and our bodies are slicked with sweat, and my back is scored from her nails, I bury myself deep and come so hard I see stars.

We lie there a few minutes, breathless, caught in the kind of intimate tangle I could live in forever. But the rubber's got to go. Reluctantly I unravel our limbs and, crawling off the bed, drop a single kiss to her breast. When I return from the bathroom, Julia lifts the sheet for me to climb back in.

She rests her fingertips over my heart as we lie there. "That was as close to having sex without a condom as I've ever come."

I press my hand over hers, holding it there. "Me too. Was it okay that we did it?"

She nods, her smile shy. "More than okay. And umm, just so you know, I've been on the pill longer than I've been having sex."

I gently brush back a few strands of golden blonde hair that have fallen into her face. She's got to be thinking about all the bullshit the press puts out about me. The different women, the player reputation. That hasn't been me for a long time, but even when it was— "I've always been safe, always been tested, so you don't need to worry."

She gives me a contented yawn. "I'm not worried. I

know you would never do anything that put me at risk. I trust you. More than any guy I've ever been with."

I trust her, too. In too many ways to count.

"You know what I'm thinking about?" she asks around a satisfied sigh.

"My recovery time? How long before I can do that to you again?"

I'm pretty sure she was trying to give me a playful swat, but now she's feeling me up, and there's not much in this world that feels better than the lazy exploration of her fingers over my chest and stomach.

"High school."

Makes sense. "Wishing you'd let me kiss you that last night after all, huh?" All this time we could have been together. Hell, by now she'd probably be—

"I'm thinking about your mom's van."

Okay, so much for connecting on a level where we share each other's thoughts. Clearly that's bullshit, because my mom's 2002 minivan was seriously the last place my mind would have gone. "Umm, what about it?"

"That van was parked outside the school at 2:35 every school day, your mom fidgeting in the front seat and then practically peeling out of the lot once you were in the car."

Yeah, she's a little intense. I should probably call her this week. "Had to get me to practice. It was kind of a haul."

"Yeah. But what was always crazy to me was after

126

the draft. After the signing bonus, even that last night when you met me at the lagoon, you showed up in that van. You could have bought yourself an Escalade or a Hummer, but you were still driving your mom's *teal* van." Stacking her hands over my chest, she rests her chin on top. "You paid off your parents' mortgage, but you didn't get yourself a new car."

"I guess it seemed like the right thing to do. I mean, Julia, the sacrifices they made so I'd have the opportunities I did—moving to Bearings sophomore year? They gave up jobs and friends and a house they loved so I'd be within driving distance of a Tier 1 team. My mom drove ninety minutes each way to get me to those practices." I run my hand over the silky strands of her hair. "What's got you thinking about that stuff?"

She smiles, but there's almost something bittersweet about it. "I didn't give you enough credit when you were leaving. You kept saying us being friends wasn't going to change because you were going into the NHL. You dropped me at home that last night, and I went into my room and cried because I was so sure it was the last time I'd talk to you."

I remember what it was like saying goodbye to her.

I was terrified about going to Dallas. Worried I was going to fail and that all the things I'd given up over the years—parties, dances, prom, relationships that required a commitment I'd already made to my sport, college—would be for nothing.

Julia looked me in the eye that night and told me

she believed in me. That I was going to make it. But that even if somehow things didn't work out—I would never have to wonder what might have been if I'd given that much more. I'd given everything I had, and she was proud of me. It was what I'd needed to hear from my best friend, and in that moment, I'd wanted her to be more. Of course, she shut me down with a consolation IOU, one that's paid off pretty well, based on the fact that we're both lying in bed naked. But I still can't believe she thought I'd disappear on her.

"Julia, it kills me to think of you like that. Especially considering I had to force myself to wait to call you when I got there."

Her head pops up, shock in her eyes. "What?"

"I didn't want you to think I was some wuss, too chickenshit to make it a day in the big leagues without needing to check in with his emotional support buddy."

That earns me another one of those swat-feel combos. Then she's shaking her head.

"You're a really good guy, Greg."

I cough. Wrapping my arm snugly around her, I flip her over so I'm on top. "Julia, we've known each other for thirteen years. You're only figuring this out *now*?"

She laughs, and the sound makes everything okay. "No! No. I've always known it. I just wish I didn't always doubt the good things."

Peering down into her soulful eyes, I promise, "You'll never have to doubt me."

# Chapter 13

*Greg*

*L*ET'S GO OUT," I suggest, kissing my way down Julia's neck to the little spot I discovered a few weeks back. The one that gets me results of the breath-catching, eyes-hazing, lip-biting variety. "I want to buy you a giant breakfast with waffles and bacon and whipped cream. Fresh-squeezed orange juice and too many cups of coffee. Late practice today, so I'm off until four. We could take a walk down by the lake."

She smiles, moaning softly when I flick my tongue against her skin. "Food sounds great, *especially the whipped cream*, but what do you think the chances are of getting all that ordered in?"

I press my brow to her shoulder and breathe. It was worth the ask.

It's been a month since Julia and I started sneaking around in earnest, and truth be told, I'm surprised we haven't gone public yet. Initially, it made sense to be cautious. She wanted to make sure this thing between us stuck. But it's *good* with us.

And I'm not talking about the sex, which is also fucking good. Seriously, hot as sin.

What I'm getting at is, it's more than that. The full package.

We talk. We tease. We bicker and debate and trash-talk and fall into bed laughing on the nights we're in town together.

We order late-night takeout, and once, after I was gone for a six-day stretch, we even tried to cook dinner together. It was pathetic, and I had to throw out half a set of ruined cookware, but when the smoke cleared and the fire alarm was silenced, it was just the two of us in each other's arms, laughing so hard we could barely stand. When we finally caught our breath, I looked into her smoke-reddened eyes and it hit me square in the center of my chest.

This woman couldn't be more perfect for me if I'd scribbled one of those wish lists and set it on fire to let the ashes float up to God himself.

I want to take her out. Show her off.

I want Rux to stop talking about how hot she is.

I want Natalie to come over and give me all her relentless little sister shit in front of her, just so I get to hear Julia laugh a little more.

I want to take her to my mom's for our traditional not-on-actual-Christmas Christmas dinner.

I want to go to one of her football games and make sure all those players who keep asking her out know she's mine and that they should try answering her questions like fucking professionals.

Jesus, I want to take a walk with her.

But more than any of that, I want her to want it too.

Her fingers thread through my hair, sliding around in that way that almost feels as good as sex. "Are you mad that I don't want to take things public?"

I pull back to meet her eyes. "No. No way, Jules. And it's not like we're talking about waiting forever here, right?"

The tiniest wince flashes across her face, and I can't quite believe she hasn't filled this pause that's stretching a little too long with assurances.

I clear my throat. "You're protective of your career. I respect that. But it's not like I'm in the NFL."

"No, but you're a pro athlete, and that's enough to get people talking."

"Maybe, but at some point, that's a bridge you have to be willing to cross." I need her to hear me. "This isn't a fling, and I'm not going anywhere."

Again, there's a flash of vulnerability in her eyes. I lean closer, gentling my tone. "It's you and me. We know each other in ways that put us past casual before we even crossed the first line."

"I know. And of course I'm planning to cross that bridge with you. I am." Snagging the sheet that's draped across my waist, she wraps it around hers like a sarong as she slips out of bed topless. "It's about timing."

Damn. My eyes fix on her breasts as she gathers her hair above her head and clips it into a messy knot.

It's a cheap tactic, and I know she's trying to distract me.

She's not ready. I said I'd be cool about it, and for her, I will be.

So I soak in the sight of her beautiful body and let the rest go.

---

*Julia*

I'm in New York to meet with my agent, Joanne Peets. It's gone from an afternoon meeting to a meeting and a drink and now to a meeting, drink, and dinner. It's exciting that she's got so many opportunities to talk about and ideas for upping my recognition beyond the sideline reporting. And while I'm honored to be invited to speak at my alma mater and present an award at a literacy benefit, I can't help but wish she had something for me with more long-term potential.

We're finishing our braised lamb appetizer when I hear a familiar voice from behind me.

"Well, if it isn't two of my very favorite girls in the world."

"Mike!" Joanne beams over my shoulder and quickly stands to meet him.

I follow that adoring look and, sure enough, find Mike Rylan, NFL superstar, walking up behind us.

He pulls Joanne in for a hug, and then, before I can think to defend against it, he's got me too. It's awkward and uncomfortable and I do my best to get out of his hold without acting like the guy has the plague. Eventually he lets me go, looking down at me with the kind of smile that says he hasn't been put off in the slightest. As if to underscore the point, he quietly says, "Adorable," before releasing me completely.

I don't find this cute at all, especially considering the attention Mike attracts. There are phones out all around us, eyes turned from every direction, and I recognize both his name and mine carrying like a wave through the restaurant.

I turn to Joanne. "How do you guys know each other?"

Another agency represents Mike, so that's not the connection.

"I worked with Stockert & Gibbs on a joint project a few months back," Mike says.

Right. I nod as they talk about the success of the promotion. How his agent is doing and how cute her assistant's new baby is. Joanne flags a waiter to bring a chair over for Mike to join us, and I'm wondering what the hell she's thinking.

"Joanne, I'm sure Mike has other plans." I smile like it's my job, because it is. "We don't want to keep you from your night."

He shakes his head. "It was drinks, and they're through. But if you don't mind, I'd love to join you for dinner."

Joanne is throwing out her arms like she just won the lottery, and I'm starting to have serious doubts about our future together. She knows about my rules. She understands the issue of perception. And while this wouldn't be even close to a date, she should recognize that being seated at the same table as Mike Rylan is going to raise eyebrows.

It's going to mean another heart-to-heart with Ray Hettler and some kind of fallout at work. It always does.

"Mike, that's *wonderful*. We're mostly through with the business talk anyway, so your timing is perfect." Casting him another adoring smile, she adds, "As always."

This isn't the way the night was supposed to go. I was going to catch an evening flight back to Chicago, but I pushed it because Joanne asked for more time. Now the backstabber is dabbing her mouth with her napkin and excusing herself to make a quick call. Leaving me alone with Mike.

I make a mental note to call the M. McCalister

Agency tomorrow and set up a meeting, not that it will help me tonight. Especially when Mike rests a hand on my shoulder and leans in for a conspiratorial whisper.

"So, here's your shot, Julia. Ask me anything you want to know."

There are easily a hundred questions I could rattle off without missing a beat, the first of which would be about the shoulder he's been favoring. But it doesn't feel right. I don't want to use the fact that Mike's interested in me to get information out of him, and more than that, I don't want to give him the idea I'm interested myself. I'll save those questions for a call when there's no misunderstanding the context.

I excuse myself, confident that the minute I leave, Joanne will swoop back in.

The ladies' room is like a mini-spa complete with a trickling waterfall built into one wall, a small lounge area, and a young woman offering a neck massage. All I want is privacy, so I take the seat in the far corner and text Greg.

**Me: I think I need a new agent.**

His reply is immediate.

**Greg: Why? Still not finding you the right opportunities?**

Why.

I think about Mike sitting at our table. It's not really something I can explain over a text, and calling is out of the question. You never know who's within earshot.

**Me: Not really. I'm thinking maybe she isn't as serious about my plans as I am.**

At least not about the rules I've been very clear about with her. She doesn't have to agree with them, but she does have to abide by them.

**Greg: Would a dick pic make you feel better?**

I cough out a laugh, and find the attendant hovering a few feet away, offering a glass of water with a cucumber floating in it.

"No thank you."

**Me: Always.**

A second later, my phone pings with a black-and-white picture of Dick Van Dyke, and two seconds after that, Andy Dick, this one in the *Hey, Girl* style. It has me laughing so hard I don't even care that one of the players I interview on the field is sitting at my dinner table.

**Me: You make me smile.**

**Greg: You make me hot.**

**Greg: And you make me smile.**

**Greg: Miss you.**

Two words. So simple. But I feel them deep in my heart.

**Me: You too.**

**Greg: When does your flight get in?**

**Me: 3 a.m.**

If I'd had any idea how quick Joanne would be to

give up our meeting, I would have taken my original flight and gotten in early enough to see him.

**Greg: Come here from the airport. Park in the garage. I'll have Erwin give you a key to get in.**

I stare at the small screen in my hand. His building is about as private and secure as it gets. The attendants in the garage and lobby must have signed some kind of blood oath involving their firstborns, because Greg essentially said we could have sex on the security desk and never have to worry about the guard breathing a word of it.

It's why we always go to his apartment instead of mine. The garage is private and requires a key code to enter.

And with only seven tenants in the building, running into someone in the lobby damn near never happens. Even if we did, running into them at one p.m. is a lot different, not to mention easier to explain away, than getting busted for what smacks of booty-call o'clock.

**Greg: See how you feel when you get in. The key will be downstairs either way.**
**Me: I've got to get back. Have a good night.**

I nearly type those three forbidden words. Lately, they seem to be constantly on the tip of my tongue, but I can't say them. Not yet. Not even when I've known they were real for weeks. I… I need to be careful.

When the night ends, Joanne signals for the check, and Mike shakes his head.

"Sorry, Joanne. Hope you don't mind, but I already got it."

She puts on a delighted scowl. "You know better than that, Mike."

He laughs and, to my horror, slings an arm around my shoulder.

"You know I've been trying to get Julia here to let me buy her dinner forever. I figured this was my best chance." He squeezes my shoulder and gives me another dimple-laced smile that has my stomach churning. "Though hopefully next time I won't have to hijack a business meeting with her agent to do it."

"Mike," I start, pulling away from his hold, no nonsense in my eyes.

He holds up a hand. "Yeah, yeah. I know. You don't date athletes."

"It's not—"

"I won't be playing forever."

Before I have a chance to reply, he drops a kiss on my cheek and says good night.

When he's safely out of earshot, I level Joanne with a killing look. "What was that?"

She folds one hand over the other on the table and gives me a calculating smile. "The kind of PR you can't buy."

## Chapter 14

*Greg*

MY MUSCLES BURN in the satisfying way of being pushed hard, and despite the cacophony of noise around the weight room—mostly Vsev bitching in heated Russian about God knows what—I'm grinning like I felt up my first girl. Only waking up to Julia slipping into my bed around four this morning beats the hell out of getting up close and personal with Nancy Holtz's stuffed bra.

Julia and I didn't talk.

I didn't try to shag her.

She snuggled into me, her back to my chest, and let out this contented sigh that sounded like all the things a guy could want. Everything that mattered.

It about killed me, leaving this morning when I knew she'd be in my bed for another hour. But hell, maybe I'll be able to talk her into staying over after the game tonight. I know better than to try to talk her into actually coming to my game, but hopefully that'll change soon.

I sit back on the bench and run a towel over my face and chest as I pull out my phone to look her up on social media. I like seeing the candids the press and fans catch when she's at the airport or paying for coffee.

The first pictures come up, and they're not of Julia seated by herself with an issue of *Sports Illustrated* in her lap. Not even close.

I jerk to my feet, spilling my water over the gym floor.

"Baxter, you okay, man?" the trainer asks from where he's working with Popov.

No. I am not all right. Because all I'm getting as I scroll further and further down the feeds are pictures of Julia with Mike Rylan—the two of them seated alone at a table for dinner. Mike with his hand on the small of her back as they stand. Mike with his fucking mouth pressed against Julia's temple, her eyes closed and a half smile on her lips—the captions calling them the NFL's cutest couple.

It's not what it looks like.

The rational part of my brain knows that.

She doesn't date athletes, and never in my life have I been more pleased about what a fucking stickler she is for that rule. Except that's not exactly true, because she most definitely *does* date athletes. She's dating me.

Why didn't she tell me about this?

"Dude, you look like you're about to hurl." Rux is standing beside me, totally in a position to be able to see what was on the screen. But if he did, he isn't showing it. "Need me to hold your hair or rub your back?"

A couple of the guys laugh, and I want to, but it's not happening. Not until Julia gives me a reason to laugh.

"Back in a minute."

---

*Julia*

MY PHONE HAS BEEN GOING off for the last thirty minutes, but I'm stuck in Ray's office, assuring him the rumors aren't true.

"The audience isn't going to like the idea of you and one of the players together. Whether it's true or not, it's about perception, Julie."

My already tense stomach knots even tighter. I know. The last thing I need is Hettler driving it home for me.

"You have to be more careful than this. You have to be smarter." He leans closer, and I wonder if he's even aware that his eyes have dropped to my chest. "In this business, you can't afford to stop thinking about your future for even one careless second."

"Ray, believe me, I understand. I'll be more careful going forward."

I don't bother explaining that Joanne set me up, thinking she was doing me a favor. I need to get out of here and call Greg. I've been in Ray's office from before I even realized what was happening, so I haven't been able to check my phone. But I'd be willing to bet at least one of the zillion alerts and notifications is from him.

I should have told him about Mike.

He's going to be furious, and he'll have every reason to be. For months I've been putting him off about going public with our relationship to preserve my reputation, and now this. I feel sick.

Outside Ray's office, my boss's assistant Agnes catches sight of me from down the hall. She yelps, her mop of dark curls bouncing as she waves me down.

My boss wants to see me, ASAP.

I try to scroll through my messages while I walk, but Agnes is talking a mile a minute about what she's heard and how she wishes Mike would ask her out.

When I walk into Bill's office, I'm wearing a mask of calm as I launch into my explanation. "It's not what it looks like."

He doesn't even look up. "Of course it's not. Sit down."

Two hours pass before I leave.

My head is spinning, but at least I'm finally able to use my phone. There are too many messages to sort through, but when I get to Greg's, I see he's attached a particularly incriminating snap from the night before. It looks like I'm melting into a tender kiss Mike is planting on my brow. It looks like the kind of moment caught between two people who are more than friends and have been for some time. It looks like any number of legitimate moments between Greg and me, that no one has a chance to see because we hide them so thoroughly behind closed doors.

It looks like anything other than what it is... me, cringing beneath a kiss I wasn't prepared to defend against and praying the moment would pass without blowing up in my face.

My hands shake as I call Greg.

Voicemail. He's not answering.

I close my eyes and let a slow breath out through my nose. Is this when he's going to walk away, when he's going to leave?

No. He wouldn't do that. This is *Greg*.

He had practice today and some meetings scheduled through the afternoon, so I'm not going to flip out that he didn't answer my call. I'll text, and when he's free, we'll talk.

**Me: It's not what it looks like. I'm sorry.**

For a guy who can't answer the phone, he's pretty quick to text back.

**Greg: It looks like you were at dinner with Mike Rylan.**

**Greg: Which is weird, because I asked how dinner with Joanne went and you didn't mention it.**

Why didn't I tell him about Mike? Why didn't I explain what happened and tell him how pissed off it made me?

Because I was hoping I wouldn't have to. That I could avoid the whole thing.

Pretend it wasn't happening.

I dial Greg again, and this time, he picks up.

"I'm guessing the reason it took you hours to respond is you've been doing some kind of damage control?"

His words are clipped and cool. It's almost like he's turned away from the phone while he's talking to me.

"I've been in meetings since before I even knew what happened. But as to damage control—" he is not going to like this, "—that isn't exactly what's going on."

"What are you talking about?" And now he's back, his voice sounding closer. More urgent. "Why haven't I seen a denial on this yet? I've been watching your feeds all morning."

I swallow.

"They've been in touch with Mike, and they don't want any denials or explanations until tomorrow afternoon. Then timed, scripted replies."

There's silence from the other end of the line, and I

can all but imagine Greg opening his mouth and then closing it again. His hand working through that wild mane of his.

"I don't like it," I say quietly, moving through the halls as I talk. Unwilling to give anyone the chance to hear more than a word or two of my conversation.

"But you didn't tell them no. You didn't explain that you have a *boyfriend*, or barring that, that you've spent your entire career sacrificing your personal life to ensure this very thing didn't happen, to defend against the very *perception* they're fostering by leaving this out there for twenty-four hours."

My steps slow, and I stop. "No. I didn't. This is my career, Greg. If I'm too careless to avoid situations like this, then I have to be prepared to deal with the fallout, whatever form it takes. And in this case, it's test marketing. They want to see how the audience responds to a… softer, more accessible Julia Wesley."

I don't know what I'm expecting. Greg to blow up or hang up or tell me it's over.

But instead, he lets out a long breath. "They're going to love it. They're going to eat it up. Fucking Mike Rylan, the face of the NFL, and Julia Wesley, the sharp beauty no one but the best could win."

"No, Greg. That's not how it's going to go. They won't take it that far."

He laughs, but it's quiet, like he's pulled the phone away again. "Wanna bet?"

I bite my lip, waiting a painful beat before asking, "Are we okay?"

"Yeah, Jules. We're okay."

---

*Greg*

I'M A PRETTY LEVEL-HEADED GUY. Most of the time. Fine, I've got a temper, but it's generally quick to cool. Unfortunately, this shit with Julia and Mike today is only getting worse. It's getting close to game time, and we're facing off against the Epics tonight and that fucker Vaughn Vassar who's been up in my grill since we were fifteen years old. But that's not where my head is. Yeah, I'm definitely working through plays and thinking about what the coaches pointed out during video, but every few minutes some other trainer or guy on the team is coming up to ask me about Julia and Mike. To point out how fucking hot she is. Because we're *friends*.

Yep. I know.

Fortunately for them, me, and the team in general, most people seem to catch on to my negative, possibly threatening vibe before saying anything more.

I rub the back of my neck and do some breathing exercises at my stall. I should have used my break this afternoon to talk to Julia in person. Not like I got any sleep, going home to a bed that smelled like her.

She probably wouldn't have been able to meet up with me anyway. Can't be seen getting into Baxter's car when she's dating Rylan.

Fuck.

I drive my fist against the wall in my stall, leaving my knuckles flat, until something wings past my ear and tumbles into my space.

Picking up the tampon, I turn to the locker room and take another square to the nose. "What the hell, Rux?"

The fucker is standing a careful six feet back, holding what looks like a half dozen plastic-wrapped weapons of feminine protection.

"You shedding your uterine lining or something, Baxter?"

He's waiting for an answer, and the fact that he's confronting me is a big deal. But where the fuck did he get all those tampons? It sure as hell wasn't the Slayers' locker room.

"Look, I don't know what's going on with you, but get your shit together. We got a game." Rux being Rux, he tucks the handful into his breezers and cocks his head. "Unless whatever crawled up your crack'll actu-ally up your game. Will it? Does being pissed as fuck make you play better? 'Cause if your rage is actually like some secret advantage, then hell, I could probably knock you in the teeth a couple times before each game. I mean, I wouldn't like it. Or maybe I would. Whatever. All I'm sayin' is I'm a team fuckin' player."

Jesus. He's grinning like a fool, but not even that's enough to put out the fire in my chest. "What a giver."

"That's what your sister—" He cuts off, acting like he barely caught himself before crossing the unspoken line regarding Nat, when we both know it was just another jab, trying to get me to react. Vent off some steam. But it's not working. I'm still thinking about the clip someone dug up from an entertainment site interview with Rylan a few months back where he admits to a longstanding crush on Julia. The guy's making a play for her because he doesn't even know she's taken.

I fucking hate it.

I finish getting dressed, cranking my laces tight and pulling on my pads and jersey. I tape my stick, telling myself it's time to leave this shit with Julia behind.

Only, it's still with me when I step onto the ice to warm up, and when I blow around the rink, pushing fast and hard beneath the swirling spotlights and blaring music. It's with me as I fire puck after puck into the net.

Rux sees it too.

The game's about to start, and he cuts me a look devoid of any humor. "Whatever it is, man, let it go and get your head in the game."

"I know." Head in the game. I fucking know.

Chapter 15

*Julia*

*I*'M WORKING LATE with the rest of the crew, doing my best not to look up the Slayers game every five seconds when I'm supposed to be preparing to cover my own game this week. I've already watched two of the home team's last games and have a third queued up, but my head isn't in it. I'm rewinding the footage again when I look over the wall of my cube and see Darnell and Izzy watching the Slayers Epics game. They don't cover hockey, so this is just for fun. Their hands are up as they rock back in their seats amid a flurry of hoots and laughs.

I call to Darnell, "Who you talking about?"

He angles his head my way but keeps his eyes on the game. "Slayers. Baxter's got some shit going on."

My stomach lurches, and I have to draw on all my calm to not give anything away. "He's starting fights?"

Darnell scoffs. "Nah. He's running his mouth, but he's too smart to throw the first punch."

Izzy laughs, shaking his head. "He's sure as shit finishing them, though."

I circle around to Izzy's cube, planning to only watch a few minutes. But then I'm pulling up a chair and accepting a bottle of water from Izzy's drawer as Greg skates over to the penalty box for the third time.

Guilt gnaws at me as I watch him pull off his helmet and glare out at the ice, eyes hard, aggression visible with every breath.

This is my fault. I put my career before everything else, and now his career is taking a hit because of it.

The fighting stops midway through the second period, and Greg makes up for it by scoring two points in the third for the win, but I still feel sick with guilt.

I text him after the game to ask if I can come by. I only need to hold my breath for a few seconds.

**Greg: My place. Be waiting for me.**

---

I'M GETTING a glass of water when the door opens and slams shut from the front entry.

"Greg?"

I don't even make it out of the kitchen before he's

there, filling up the arched doorway with his broad shoulders and powerful arms.

His eyes lock with mine, and he loses his jacket, leaving him in a pair of expertly cut suit pants, a hand-stitched shirt, and an aqua tie that some personal shopper matched to his eyes. His shirt pulls across the bulk of his chest with every breath and stretches over the flexing mass of his biceps. He's gorgeous and vibrating with the kind of intensity that is both exciting and intimidating all at once.

"I saw your game."

"I saw Mike's interview." Greg's jaw flexes, and I swear the bulk of his upper body gets even bigger.

"I didn't know that was out there, but it doesn't matter. Tomorrow, we'll make our statements and it'll be over."

Greg's nostrils flare, and he crosses the kitchen in less than three strides. His big hands close around my waist, and before I can do more than let out a yelp of surprise, he's got me lifted onto the polished steel island.

"I don't want to talk about him." His hands move over my hips and up my waist, his thumbs brushing my nipples through the Slayers T-shirt I took from his drawer.

The contact has my breath hitching and my body warming in anticipation.

I slide my fingers into the dark strands of his hair, but Greg shakes them off and takes my wrists in each hand to press them back on the countertop at either side of me.

Leveling me with a hard look, he says, "We need to talk."

"Greg," I whisper, my voice breaking. "I know there's been a lot to deal with lately. And now this thing with—"

"Are we together?" The question lands heavily between us. No teasing. Nothing playful in his tone.

"Yes." He knows that, but he's still asking. The most unrelentingly confident man I've ever met needs to hear me say it. "We're together. Absolutely."

His hands find mine on the counter beside me, giving them the slightest press. A reminder not to move.

He wants control.

My eyes connect with his, and my breath catches at the dark heat I find in them.

It makes my heart skip a beat, and suddenly my nerves are tangling up with the need I feel every time we're together.

"Here's the thing, Julia. It's driving me fucking crazy that no one knows it but me. That outside these walls, what we have doesn't exist."

"That's not true. Greg, please."

"'Please' is a good start." The corner of his mouth curves, but it's not the same mischievous smile he's so famous for. It's something darker, and it calls to a part of me I didn't even know was there.

"I'm going to need to hear you say that a few times tonight."

"I'll say it as many times as you want to hear it."

He takes the hem of my shirt and pushes it up, so the soft fabric bunches above my breasts. Then, dragging his knuckle across the low-cut lace edging of my bra, he nods. "Yes, you will."

Again, there's that edge to his tone, and my body responds with a needy pang.

Slipping a finger into the cup of my bra, he teases my nipple, brushing back and forth until it's hard and aching.

"Please, Greg."

He looks up from where he's playing with me. A half smile on his lips.

"That sounds like a pity *please*, Jules. I want the real ones."

He slips another finger into the cup, catching my nipple between them with a firm hold. My breath catches, and liquid heat spills through my center as my hips begin to move.

He plays with me like that, his hot gaze shifting from my eyes to my mouth to where his skilled fingers are driving me wild. When he's had enough, his hands skim lower, over my belly and down to my stretchy yoga pants.

A nudge, and I raise my hips for him to pull them off my legs, leaving me in my panties, the bra that's barely covering me, and the shirt bunched above. I might have felt exposed like this, maybe silly sitting on the counter like an item on display, but the way Greg is looking at me leaves me burning hot.

"Pull down your bra, and touch yourself like I am." He squeezes my nipple tighter, giving it a tug as I reach for the other cup, my fingers trembling. I do as he says, too excited to do anything but comply. Eagerly. The men I've dated before would never talk to me like this. I wouldn't want them to. But with Greg, I hope there's more he wants from me, because I love giving it to him.

He gives my nipple another tweak, harder than before, and need, sharp and pointed, spears through me. Before I can even think, the plea spills past my lips. "Greg, *please*."

Another one of those darkly satisfied smiles as his eyes hold with mine. "That's more like it."

I pinch and pull, mimicking his touch as best I can, turned on beyond belief by the idea that what I'm doing pleases him.

He pulls me closer to the edge of the counter and, standing between my legs, leans in to kiss me. I'm expecting something on the rougher side to match the way he's playing with my breasts, but it's soft. More about the teasing slide of his lips against mine than the crush of possession. This claim is seductive and slow, and it makes me want to beg for more. To beg him to take. To beg him to let me give him everything, all that I have.

When his tongue slips past my lips, a shudder tears through me, and I moan around the taste of him.

My legs are open, my knees clutching at his sides as we work my nipples to the point where pleasure crests inside me with every pull, pinch, twist, and tug. All the while he's totally in control, thrusting deep into my mouth, taking my escalating need and building it higher.

When he pulls back, I try to follow him.

"Greg." I run my tongue over my sensitive lips, aching for more. "*Please*."

He smiles against my lips. "Now you're just spoiling me."

Then he's brushing my hand aside so he has control of both breasts. Cupping them together in his big hands, he bows his head so his hair dusts across my chest as he licks from one tender mound to the other. Drawing the straining bud into the warmth of his mouth, he sucks hard.

"Greg, please! *Please*!"

I'm met with a low growl and the tightening of his grip.

My hands are in his hair, the dark strands spilling out from between my trembling fingers. It's erotic and emotional and overwhelming in all the ways I associate with this man.

Releasing his hold on my breasts, he runs his hands blissfully lower. I'm aching, and even though he's standing between my legs, I need more. I want him to grab my ass and haul me against his straining fly. I want him to rock into the needy spot between my legs and take me so hard on the countertop that I won't even be able to look at it again without coming.

"Julia," he growls against my neck, his fingers tracing the lace edging of my panties from the sides, down the front of the leg holes, to where they're soaked between us. "Tell me you're my girl."

I'm barely able to form the words. "I'm your girl."

His thumb slides beneath the slick panel, barely grazing my folds as he pulls away from the heat of my pussy. Cool air teases the overheated skin, and I moan.

"Wider, Jules."

My heart skips, and I do as he asks to make room for him.

Then he's got both hands wrapped in that panel, pulling it tight around my hips and through the back, making me aware of what he's about to do.

He meets my eyes and I give him what he's waiting for.

"*Please.*"

The fabric shreds within his grasp, and my inner muscles clench with anticipation.

He's standing in front of me still fully dressed, his shirt open a single button at his neck, but otherwise tucked in beneath his belt and suit pants. My rugged gentleman.

I've never seen anything so sexy in all my life.

He steps back, and I imagine he's about to start to

strip. Instead he runs his hand over the hard bulge of his cock, moving up and down the length in a slow, firm stroke that has me squirming where I sit. His eyes are fixed between my legs where my panties hang in shreds, leaving me open and exposed to him.

With any other man, I'd be shy, embarrassed. Trying to cover up. But with Greg, I'm starved for his eyes on me.

"Tell me what you want, Jules."

I love the way he's always saying my name. No baby or babe or sexy or any other pet name as inter-changeable as the women he's used it with before. Like he doesn't ever forget that he's with me. Julia. His Jules.

I follow the movement of his hand and imagine him sliding into me. "I want you inside me."

"That all? Just me pushing up inside you nice and slow and gentle? That's what you want?"

He knows as well as I do it isn't. When I shake my head, he demands, "Then what? Tell me. I want to hear the words from that pretty mouth."

He's gripping his shaft through his pants now, the fine fabric outlining how long and thick he is.

I lick my lips. I need it.

"I want it hard. I want you to… fuck me. I want you to make me feel it. Everywhere."

His hand stops moving, and I blink up to his eyes. I've never seen them so dark. So hot.

He steps back into the space between my legs,

pushing the scrap of my panties aside to brush his thumb up the length of my sex.

When he gets to the top, he rubs my slickness around and around in slow circles until I'm shaking, jerking into the contact, giving up one "please" after another in a steady desperate stream.

"You know what *I* want?"

I shake my head. "Tell me."

Make it as dirty as possible.

"I want Mike fucking Rylan to stop telling the world how into you he is."

I gasp, my eyes shooting to his. His fingers haven't stopped playing with me, the contact only intensifying.

"I want you to tell him to back off because you have a boyfriend." He's dragging me closer and closer to the edge with his touch. Making me fight off my pleasure as I struggle with the words that are breaking my heart.

"Greg," I start.

"I want to go online and see the picture someone caught of *us*. I want the look in your eyes to have been exactly what it appears to be." He slides a finger into me, long and thick, pulls out, and then pushes back in with two. "I want to see a poll guessing how many months *we've* managed to keep our affair a secret, and not one showing that ninety-three fucking percent of those asked think you and Mike would make a perfect couple."

"Greg, please."

He shakes his head, giving me a stern look as his fingers flex and spread inside me, stroking over that spot that makes me crazy.

I can't let him make me come like this. I can't find release in all the ways I've hurt him.

"I *don't* want to give you what you want, because not having what I want is fucking killing me." He strokes into me one last time, pushing me to the very edge of coming, but then somehow holds me back from tipping over.

He pulls his hands from between my legs and brings his fingers to his mouth to suck. God.

"You're so fucking sweet, Jules."

Then his hands are going to his belt and he's undoing his fly. I'm teetering on the brink of release, but all that matters to me is how my choices have affected this man.

"Greg—"

"Tell me you're mine. Even if no one else knows, I want to hear it."

"I am."

"Tell me your heart is mine."

"It is." More than I can admit.

"Your body."

Completely. "Yes."

His cock is out, pulsing an angry red as he rolls on a condom from his wallet. He lines up with my opening and grits his teeth. "*This.*"

"Yes."

He pushes inside, and I cry out, contracting around him as he stretches me wide.

"Greg!"

"When you come, it's mine."

I'm nodding, but it's not enough. Not what he wants. "Say it," he demands, shoving inside me until he bottoms out and I cry, "Yes!"

"Julia, I'm going fucking insane. I know that if I wait, eventually it's going to work itself out. I know that I'm throwing a tantrum, and it's not fair, and I'm jealous, and it's bullshit. But after seeing you with that other guy, knowing that he fully intends to try and win you... because *he doesn't even know about me*, I need to hear you begging for me, coming apart with my name on your lips, because no one else makes you feel the way I do. Because you belong to me."

He's shafting inside me, full length. Thrusting so deep, he meets the edge of all I can take.

He's giving me everything. *Everything.*

"You're mine, Julia."

"Yes!"

Our eyes lock, and he can see it's true. He knows it as surely as I do.

His movements become faster, his muscles tensing, until my name rips past his lips as he comes.

We're quiet and still, the sounds of our breathing filling the silence around us.

Brow pressed against my chest, he says, "That's good. Because I'm yours."

## Chapter 16

*Julia*

HEAVY TRAVEL IS part of the gig, for both of us. Minimum, I'm gone three days a week. And for the most part, I love it. But not so much right now. The Slayers had a seven-night road trip, and the day Greg got home, my flight out left thirty minutes before they touched down. We've been talking and texting, but it's not the same as touching. Sharing the same space and breathing the same air. Being able to reach out and press my hand against his chest so I can feel his heartbeat.

I'm tucked into the wingback by the window in my generic hotel room, my laptop open with my notes from talking with the Raiders players and coaches this afternoon. My phone is resting in my lap, my head-phones plugged in for our video call.

"Rux is probably going to miss a game," Greg says from the tiny window. "But the team doc doesn't think it'll be more than one."

"I'm glad it isn't worse. That hit was brutal."

He nods, and even through the phone I can see how his eyes harden. He's pissed about his friend being out for a game from a cheap shot thrown by a guy on the other team. It actually hurts to see him upset like this and know that I can't go to him. I won't be able to wrap my arms around him or sift my fingers through the overgrown waves of his hair for another few days.

"I miss you." It's like an ache in my heart that's only getting worse with every day that passes. And as much as I look forward to the texts, phone and video calls, I hurt even more after saying goodbye.

"I miss you too. Like you wouldn't believe." He looks around to make sure he's alone, then leans closer to the screen. "I actually looked up flights last night. Thinking I could get there and get back before the next practice."

"So what happened? Airfare too steep for the cool fifteen mil they're paying you?"

He laughs, shaking his head.

"Coach called a meeting, and I couldn't make it work without risking missing practice."

At this level, players don't miss practice. Ever.

We talk a few minutes more, he makes me laugh hard enough I have tears in the corners of my eyes, and

I flash my bra at him before we say goodbye. Couple more days and I'll be back in his arms. In his bed.

Couple more days. No big deal.

———

*Greg*

I AM NOT GOING to jump her at the front door.

That's what I keep reminding myself every time I check my watch to see that another thirty-seven seconds have passed and I'm that much closer to Julia getting over here.

It's been too long since I've seen her, had my hands on her, and the man downstairs has started hijacking my consciousness, planning all the ways he'd like to reconnect with her.

Up against the door.

On the floor in front of the door.

When he's feeling particularly restrained, we make it all the way to the couch before I start tearing her clothes off.

But I'm not an animal. So when Julia gets here in the next twenty minutes, I'm going to hug her. Kiss her, with tongue, but only for a minute. And then I'm going to offer her a glass of wine and ask about her flight back and the game and all the other shit I'm really interested in but can't seem to focus on because I keep thinking about taking her panties off with my mouth. Tasting her. Making her— *Easy, man.*

I'm going to offer her a glass of wine.

Any minute now.

There's a knock at my door, and I force myself to *walk* through the living room, not run.

I'm *not* an animal.

I'm not—I jerk the door open, and before I can even say hello—hell, before I can even breathe, she's launched herself at me, throwing her arms around my neck and showering my face with kisses.

I'm a big guy who takes hits from even bigger guys for a living, but the sheer force of Julia's affection knocks me back a step. But I'm quick on my feet, recovering fast, and within a heartbeat, my arms close around her like a vise, one around her back, the other across her ass. Her ankles lock behind me, and that shower of kisses slides into a single, soulful, tender, achingly sweet kiss.

It's good. It's right.

Then it's hot. And hotter.

Julia's hands are everywhere, and by the time we come up for air, we've made it less than five feet into the entry, and my apartment looks like a laundry bomb detonated in it. Julia's jeans hang precariously from the back of my couch. Her blouse is in a tattered heap surrounded by its own buttons in the corner. Her bra is under the entry table, and her panties are dangling from the coat closet's doorknob. My track pants are caught around my ankle, and my T-shirt is under her head.

That's right. I'm a fucking gentleman.

Julia brushes a bit of sweat-damp hair from her brow and smiles up at me. "Hi."

*Hi.*

Because this is the first chance we've had to say it. Because she missed me, maybe as much as missed her. Because some things are as simple as that.

Jesus. I love her.

I open my mouth to say it, but fight back the words before they get free.

She isn't ready to grab a cup of coffee with me down the street. No way she's ready to hear something like that. I touch her face as gently as I can and breathe around the emotion shoving at the walls in my chest.

Glancing off to the side, she bites her lip. "Sorry about all that. I was going to try to be cool, but…"

And then we're both laughing as I gather her up in my arms and carry her back to my bed where I toss her down with a bounce. Following that satisfying squeal, I climb in with her. She's pressed against my chest, our limbs in the kind of intimate tangle that only makes me want to get closer.

She traces her fingertips over my jaw and down my neck. "I missed you."

"Jules, our schedules make it hard enough to be

together without adding in this secretive stuff. I don't want to keep hiding that we're together."

Tucking her head into my chest, she closes her eyes. She doesn't want to talk about it. Fight about it. Whatever. But I want to get this out.

"I know it's not the same with your career as it is with mine." All I have to do to stay on top is play better than everyone else. For Julia, it's not only about the quality of her research, her ability to relay what's happening on the field, or her unparalleled knowledge of the game. It doesn't matter if she's better than everyone else… not if the right people aren't on her side. There are too many other bullshit factors to count. But even so… "Julia, it's not like you've had some string of affairs with celebrity athletes. This is one quiet relationship with a guy you've known from before either of us were in the national spotlight. No one is going to judge you for having a boyfriend."

She presses a kiss to my chest and sighs. "People judge me for how I wear my hair at the games, Greg. They write letters when I look too sexy and they write letters when I 'try to look like a man.' The only thing they don't write letters about is my love life. Because I've never had one."

I can't even begin to imagine what it must be like to be judged for something other than my merit. It pisses me off that Julia doesn't have to imagine, because she knows firsthand.

"Can we please give it a little more time?"

"Yeah, Jules, of course we can." What else can I say? I want to be with her. I just don't want to hide it.

———————

*Julia*

"THERE IS *DEFINITELY* something going on with you." Cammy sets the juice glass she was washing in the dishrack and crosses her arms. "You've got that panicky smile on your face and those weird splotches on your neck from when you're freaking out. What's up, Greg angling to plow the back fields?"

Tea spews out my nose, and Cammy nods, a satisfied smile on her face.

"What? No!"

After tossing me a rag for the table, she pulls up a chair. "Okay, then spill it."

I don't want to tell her. Saying it out loud seems somehow scarier than keeping it inside. But at the same time, something is happening within me, and I feel like I'm about to burst. Like, scary or not, I have to say the words.

"I think I'm ready."

She leans forward, brows furrowed. "Ready? Umm, didn't you say you gave up your dusty old V card to Dan Berling like a million years ago? Or, I mean, I was only joking about the back fields thing, but if that's—"

My hand is up between us, my tea pushed a safe

distance away. "I think I'm ready to go public about dating Greg."

Cammy stares, her lips parted like she's stunned into stillness.

Then slowly, she reaches for my tea and drains the mug. "Whoa, you two are really serious."

I nod. Barely able to meet her eyes. "He makes me feel things, want things I've never wanted with another guy. He makes me feel *safe*, Cammy. Like for the first time in my life, the mistake would be *not to give in*."

"Have you talked to him about going public?"

"Not really. He asked me about it when we saw each other on Monday. I put him off, but I haven't felt right since. I keep telling myself not to get carried away. Not to be rash." Not to get too invested in someone who might leave. "Not to let some guy jeopardize the life I'm building."

Cammy reaches for my hand. "Not to be like Mom? Like me?"

I swallow hard, guilt pushing at my chest. "That's not what I meant."

She smiles at me, no judgment in her eyes. "You keep telling yourself not to let him in. And?"

"And it feels like he's already there, Cammy. Like all I'm accomplishing by pretending he isn't is hurting us both."

Cammy nods and gets up from the table to grab the open bottle of white from the fridge. Sitting back down, she fills the mug between us and, eyes gleaming, offers me the first sip. "So what are you going to do?"

I laugh, because it's so very much my sister. Making the most of what's in front of her. I have a swallow, ignoring the hint of chamomile. "You know how I've been getting all those calls for interviews since the business with Mike Rylan?"

# Chapter 17

*Greg*

*I*'M WEARING A hole through the floor of my apartment.

Something's going on with Julia.

I thought everything was perfect the other night, but before she left, things changed. She turned in on herself, got distracted. I asked about it, but she waved me off like it was nothing and kissed me goodbye.

Her game was in town this week, so I thought we'd have more time together. I was looking forward to seeing her after all her pre-game meetings with the teams, coaches, and producers, but when she finally showed up, she seemed off. Twitchy. Less *my* Julia. And hell, I still don't know what to make of what happened two nights ago, when I came home from picking up dinner for us and found her whispering into her phone in my bedroom. I said her name and she jumped so high, she nearly chucked the phone across the room.

That's the sort of shit that would freak me the fuck out with any other girl. Reminding me a little too much of Shelly and all the shit I should have recognized wasn't right.

Except this is Julia. The girl I've known for thirteen years, and in all that time, who has never given me a reason not to trust her. Which means whatever is going on isn't some underhanded scheme… but it's something.

She wants me to meet her at her place this afternoon.

*Her place.*

After months of not being willing to risk someone seeing me going into her place, *now* she wants me to come over.

I may not have gone to a traditional university, but I can put two and two together. Julia isn't worried about me being seen at her place because she knows it won't happen again. She's planning to sever ties. I'm going to walk in there, and she's going to tell me she can't do it anymore, that she won't risk whatever damage her career might take if it comes out she's dating an athlete. And then she's going to tell me goodbye.

And then I don't even know what I'm going to do, because I can't fucking imagine my life without her in it.

Christ, I want to puke.

*Julia*

By the time Ronnie calls from the lobby to let me know Greg is coming up, I'm about to jump out of my skin. I've been a wreck all week, sick with worry about whether I was making the right choice. But after this morning—nothing has ever felt better than taking that leap, and now I can't wait to see him. To throw my arms around his neck and kiss him and ask him if maybe he'd like to go pick up a protein shake at the place down by the river.

The elevator doors ping and Greg steps off, looking toward the wrong end of the floor before turning to see me waiting in the hall.

I wave, but there's no missing the hard set of his eyes or the deep furrow between his brows, and my heart drops. Something's wrong.

"Greg, what happened?"

He looks around, agitated and tense. "Come on, let's get inside before anyone sees us."

By tomorrow morning it won't matter who sees us, but based on the look on his face, now isn't the time to bring that up.

He stalks into my apartment and goes clear through the living room to the kitchen before turning and stalking back.

"No Cammy or Matty?"

It almost sounds like an accusation.

"They're staying with Matty's father's family in Arizona this weekend."

A nod. "So we're alone?"

My stomach churns. "Yes?" What's going on with him? "Greg, do you want to sit down and talk?"

He shoves his fingers through his hair and gives me a level look.

He lets out a growl. "No, damn it, I don't want to sit down or be calm or civil or mature. I want you to fucking forget whatever the hell you're thinking, because it's wrong, okay? What we have is good, Jules. I don't care if we have to hide it, I really don't. But I don't want to give this up."

Give this up?

"Greg, what are you talking about?" Except then it clicks. "Wait, you think I'm breaking up with you?"

His jaw flexes once. Twice. "You're not? Then what the hell has been going on all week? And why are we *here*?"

"Greg, no. I'm so sorry. I had a big decision to make about something, and I wasn't handling it very well. But it wasn't because I didn't want to be with you. The opposite. We're here because I thought you might want to take a walk down to the river."

He's stopped moving, that agitated energy seeming to collapse in on itself. "A walk?"

"Like a date," I say, feeling inexplicably shy.

Greg's so upset, I'm about to explain about this

morning, but before I can he's crossing the room, a look in his eyes so fierce the words evaporate off my tongue.

His hands are on my face, cupping my cheeks. "You're not breaking up with me?"

He doesn't give me a chance to answer before his mouth comes down, hard and demanding. I clutch at his hair, his shirt.

Breaking away, he searches my eyes. "Fuck, I need to hear you say it."

I've never seen him so vulnerable, and I hate that I'm the one who caused it. I smooth my palms over his chest, over his shoulders and up to his face. Brushing one thumb across his heavy cheekbone, I whisper, "How could I break up with you? *I love you.*"

His breath gusts out and then he's kissing me even harder, saying my name again and again. I'm crushed against his chest, my feet lifted off the ground as he carries me to my room. We stumble into bed, and he uses his big hand to scoop beneath my back and lift me farther up.

"Say it again." He's so close, his gruff plea brushes my neck, sending chills across my skin.

"I love you. I'm *in* love with you." God, it's so easy now, I wonder how I've managed to hold the words back this long. I want to tell him more, to tell him everything. "I think I've been falling for you from the day we met. I was just too scared to give it a chance."

"Jules." His forehead presses into that spot above my heart. "I thought I was losing you."

My fingers slide into the thick waves of his hair, and tears prick at the corners of my eyes. "I'm so sorry. Feeling like this—it's new to me, and I didn't know how to handle it."

Hurting this man was the last thing I wanted to do.

His head comes up, his brow furrowed as he brushes a thumb at the far corner of my eye.

"Tears?"

"You were so upset. You thought—"

"I thought I was going to have to talk you out of a bad decision. I thought I was going to have to remind you of all the ways we work." His already deep voice goes even deeper. "I thought you were crazy if you believed I'd let you go."

Skimming my hands down the sides of his body, I gather his long-sleeved shirt, inching it up as I ask, "You wouldn't let me go?"

Shifting to his knees, he reaches overhead and pulls the shirt off in one swift motion. My mouth waters at the sight of all that hard-packed muscle and taut skin. The power in this man's body is incredible, but in that moment it's his power over my heart that overwhelms me the most.

"Never."

That's a long time. The kind of timeline I make a point not to associate with my relationships. But with Greg, *I want to believe*.

"Why not?" I ask.

He's leaning over me, his hand cupping my hip to keep us in contact. His eyes meet mine, sure and steady. "Because I love you too."

---

*Greg*

MAYBE IT's because I thought I might not have it again, but I can't get enough of her mouth. Her kiss. Her breathy sighs and soft gasps. We lose our clothes bit by bit until we're naked together, skin to skin, our limbs a tangled perfection.

"Now you say it again," she purrs, her hands sliding down my back to the top of my ass.

"I love you." She doesn't need to know that I haven't said those words since I was nineteen, and my regret over saying them then was so profound that, even nine years later, they scare the hell out of me. But this time, I understand them. I mean them.

This time it's real.

Our tongues slide around and against each other, driving us both wild.

No more waiting.

I break away, but it's not to reach for the ring of latex in my wallet. It's so I can see her beautiful face when my bare dick slides heavily down her spread seam to align with her opening.

I can tell when she registers what I'm asking.

She stills, then gives me a small nod.

"Are you sure?" I ask, holding myself back, even though I'm aching to take her. This is too important to get wrong.

Julia's answer doesn't come in words, but in the tender caress of her hands along the sides of my stubble-rough jaw and the slide of one knee up my side. Her answer is in her eyes. Fuck, the love in them—it's blinding.

This time, when I take her mouth, I take her body too.

It. Is. Amazing.

She's warm and wet, parting around me with a gentle resistance that has my moan meeting hers at the center of our kiss.

*She loves me.*

I delve deep between her legs until I bottom out, my groin meeting the spread of her sex in a flush kiss that matches our mouths. Nothing has ever felt so right.

Another flutter of her muscles around me, and I can't wait any longer.

Drawing back nearly to the head and then pushing full length inside her, I set a firm, steady rhythm between us.

She's soaked, slick, and coating me completely. I want to go slow, make it last as long as humanly possible so I can savor every wet velvety stroke. But already I feel the needy clench and pull of her body, the leading spasm signaling she's close. I could draw it out, make her wait. But I want to give her everything she needs, so I let go, hammering into that spot between us that pushes her over the edge.

"Greg!"

"Look at me," I grit out, barely hanging on. Our eyes lock. "I love you, Jules."

And she comes apart.

## Chapter 18

*Greg*

I'VE BEEN TALKING and texting and video chatting with Julia for months, so even though this is the first time I've been in her apartment, I'm actually pretty familiar with the layout and the décor. But washing up in Julia's bathroom is a different experience altogether.

It smells like her, only in a concentrated way that has me investigating the pink marble counters stacked with rows of makeup, hair stuff, and so much girlie shit I can't help but grin and reach for a little jar to see what's inside. It smells like cucumbers, and I'm pretty sure I'm going to have to go hunting for where exactly that scent resides on Julia's body. I set the jar back where it was and glance around at the rest of the frilly business, until the trash bin catches my eyes and I stop.

It's an open top, no lid, the contents clear as day, and enough to wipe that grin clean from my face.

I lean closer, not breathing as I retrieve the only item within. A circular punch pack of birth control pills. Half used.

I'm a guy who knows how to handle pressure. Who doesn't crack. But here in Julia's bathroom, less than five minutes after sharing the most meaningful moment of my life with her, my hands actually start to shake.

It's not what it looks like.

Julia isn't like Shelly.

I've known her almost half my life. I trust her.

Except now all I can think about are the pieces of this past week that haven't fit. The change in Julia. The way she couldn't always meet my eyes, and the guilt I sometimes saw when she would.

She was trying to make a decision about something big. About her future.

Jesus. There's no way this is happening again.

*Don't even think it.* But I'm already there, and the memory of ice-cold dread gripping my gut is as sharp as it was nine years ago.

Shelly looking like the sweetest, hottest thing I'd ever seen. Feeling like such a fucking man when it was *my eyes* she locked with from across the party full of pro athletes.

The way she'd stroked my ego so hard, my nine-teen-year-old self hadn't been able to see anything but her.

*"You're the best, Greg."*
*"No one can play like you."*
*"No one gets me as hot as you."*
*"I think I'm falling in love with you."*

I should have seen what she was... and what she wasn't. I should have known better.

The burn of more memories works through me. Buying her jewelry at Tiffany. Her mouth around my cock, again and again and again. Like she couldn't get enough, which was weird, considering she spit instead of swallowed. My confusion that morning I walked into the bathroom after her, needing to piss, only to find her spitting a mouthful of my jizz into that little receptacle.

The lawyers. The doctors. The coaches.

The anger. The fear. The relief.

The shame.

That had been the worst. The part that got into my head so deep, I carried it with me for years before I finally managed to work it out. That feeling of being played so effectively that I never even saw it coming.

There's no way my Julia would do that. No way.

---

*Julia*

MY EYES ARE CLOSED, my mind a mushy blissful mess as I stretch in my bed, playing over all the ways Greg told me he loved me, and the look on his face when I told him. How it felt to finally take that leap and just *trust* him.

"What the fuck is this?"

I blink, turning to the bathroom, where Greg is standing in the doorway wearing his black boxer briefs and nothing else.

He doesn't look right, but I can't quite put my finger on why, except to say I don't like it. It's like someone turned out the light inside him. His jaw is clenched, and his eyes are like icy chips.

"Greg, what's going on?" I crawl out of bed, pulling the sheet around me.

He opens his hand and within that huge palm is a crumpled sleeve of birth control pills. The ones I threw away when I got home last night.

My eyes go wide as I realize what's going on. "Greg, no." My hands come up between us as laughter bubbles up from my chest. "I know what this looks like."

"It looks like you made that decision you were wrestling with this week, Julia. And I need you to tell me right fucking now that I'm wrong."

I take a step back, feeling like I've been slapped. The bubbling laughter is gone. "You're wrong."

"Then what the hell am I holding? Because it looks like a pack of half-used birth control, with the last pill used Saturday. And today, the day we had sex without a condom for the first time, is Friday. It looks like you haven't taken these in *a week*."

Greg's barely holding it together, and while I don't like what he's insinuating, I understand what it looks like.

"This is an old pack. They aren't from this month."

When he continues to stare at me, the muscles in his jaw working overtime, I start again. "I lost my prescription about a year ago and had to get a replacement. I travel so much, I figured I'd left it in a hotel room somewhere. I wasn't actually seeing anyone, so it was no big deal. I found them yesterday when I was going through some old bags to donate. Obviously I don't need them anymore, so I threw them out."

Walking over to the bed, I open my purse and find the pack I've started carrying with me to make sure I always have them, whether I've spent the night with Greg or not. "Here. See? That's today."

We shouldn't be having this conversation. Not at all, but especially not after what we just shared. The doubt and suspicion in Greg's eyes is killing me as he fingers the missing pill space from this morning.

I wait for him to say something. To pull me into his arms and tell me he's sorry for going off the rails. Finally, he turns away and, scrubbing his hands over the back of his head, mutters, "I'm sorry."

I let go of the breath I've been holding and take a step closer. I'm about to tell him it's fine, that I want to forget the whole thing, when he adds, "Look, I believe you, but I'm kind of freaking out right now. This is *one of those things* for me."

I don't know all the details, but I've heard the rumors about a pregnancy scheme early on in Greg's career. He never talked to me about it, and I wonder if he will now.

"Just—just let me get past this." He shakes his head and almost meets my eyes but looks away at the last second. "We'll talk later."

I stand there shell-shocked, watching as he pulls on his jeans, his shirt, his shoes. The muscles in his jaw jump at regular intervals, and I can feel the tension coming off him in waves. This shouldn't be happening. It can't be happening.

For a few minutes, I swore everything was perfect.

But now I'm following Greg to my front door, taking the awkward kiss I can feel he doesn't want to give me, and watching him leave. Then I'm alone, wrapped in a sheet that smells like the man who left me while I can still feel him leaking from between my legs.

Three hours later I've showered and washed the sheets. The sun has set, and the windows are dark as I sit at the kitchen table talking to my sister in Arizona.

"That's total BS, Julia," Cammy shrieks from across the miles. I would pull the earbud from my ear, but honestly, I can't muster the energy. "You didn't even miss a pill. You didn't lie to him about anything. There wasn't any 'scare,' just a piece of trash he got the wrong idea about. He's the one who ought to be sitting there feeling like hell and begging forgiveness for jumping to a pretty shitty conclusion."

I take a deep breath and nod. I know she's right. But I also know Greg isn't some jerk. He told me he was freaking out, and I want to give him some under-standing. I want to give him a chance to calm down and come back.

"Does he even know what you did this morning?"

"No. I was going to surprise him, but…" I think about the way the afternoon played out, and my eyes start to water as I shrug. "When he comes back or calls, I'll tell him then."

She's quiet for a few seconds. "Sure, honey. He'll be really excited. He's crazy about you."

I agree, but as the hours tick by, the gnawing sense of dread in my belly grows with the certainty I made a mistake.

## Chapter 19

*Greg*

*L*EAVING LIKE I did was fucked up.

Julia didn't do a damn thing wrong. Or at least, the barely rational sliver of my consciousness that's still hanging on knows she didn't. It's the irrational part that's the problem. The part that can't let go of that sick feeling spiraling through my gut. The part that's been systematically shutting down the overloaded circuits in my brain since I found that pack of pills.

I've tried all the usual tricks to get my shit together. Got on the treadmill and pounded out the miles at a punishing pace. I did breathing exercises. I did yoga. I sat on my fucking couch and talked it out with myself.

And yet every time I think about picking up the phone or going back over there, it's like a fucking vise starts to close around my chest. Like the walls are pushing in and I can't breathe.

I don't like that Julia's alone, but I can't go back until I get my head straight, so I go to Rux's instead. He's got some of the guys over, and being around the team has always grounded me.

"You look like shit, man." Rux drops onto his couch and pats his knee. He's wearing a loose T-shirt that says EAT ME on the front, worn jeans, and enough stubble to basically be a beard. "Come sit on my lap and tell Daddy what's wrong, big guy."

When I don't move from the opposite couch, don't laugh, and don't straddle the guy's lap to remind him who's the biggest dipshit of them all, he sits back and lets out a slow breath. "Damn, man. That bad?"

I rub at the numb spot at the center of my chest. "I think it might be."

"This have anything to do with a certain sports reporter you absolutely aren't dating?" He reads my look and nods. "So we gonna talk about it or get fucked up?"

This time I do laugh.

I don't even know how many hours later it is, but Rux's place is filled with guys from the team and enough puck bunnies, I'm wondering if he went on the boards with an open call.

Everyone looks like they're having fun, but all I feel is rotten. Even half-drunk, or possibly more than half, my moment of clarity has come.

I can't stop thinking about that look of utter confusion on Julia's face earlier today, and then the hurt in her eyes when we said goodbye. I shouldn't have left like I did, but I was panicking. I shouldn't have come to Rux's, but the idea of going back was more than I could handle. I shouldn't have spent the night trying to look for answers in the bottom of a bottle when the only answer I need is probably sitting alone in her apartment wondering why the fuck she ever let me into her body like she did.

I hate it. Hate the idea of her being alone. The thought that she might be doubting what we did.

I need to call her.

Pulling out my phone, I head toward one of the back bedrooms for some privacy. I've fucked everything else up today, but the least I can do is tell her I'm sorry. Ask if I can come over and talk tomorrow morning.

Halfway down the hall, two huge hands grab my shoulders, stopping me where I am. I've had enough to drink that it takes me a step or two to steady myself, and when I do, I find Rux grinning at me, flanked by bunnies on either side.

"No way, dude. Superior players don't let their wannabes drunk dial the chick causing said wannabe's heartache."

"What?"

The bunny on the right giggles and rolls her eyes. "He's saying wait until morning to call, or whatever shit you're in with this girl will only get deeper."

I look a little closer at the girl who was talking, and Rux's arm tightens around her shoulder, pulling her in to his chest. "Nah-uh, man. Tawny's with me. But her friends, Bethie and Autumn, have been dying to distract you some."

Whoa. I'm not interested in Tawny, or anyone else for that matter. But they're right about one thing. Getting in touch with Julia while I'm trashed isn't going to help.

I hold up my hands in surrender. "You're right. I won't call."

Rux nods, but before he can push the girls on me, I cut them off.

"As nice as it would be to talk with you girls, it's going to have to be another time. I'm wiped and about to go crash in Rux's guest bedroom."

The girls put on a show of pouting, but Rux gives me a nod. "Third door on the right."

"Thanks, man."

When I get to the door, it swings open before I can even turn the knob, and another blonde stumbles into me.

"Hey, you okay?" I ask, reaching out to steady her as I try to get a look at her eyes to make sure she's all right.

She sways forward and back, and my *oh-shit* meter starts to ping. Rex has already noticed and is on his way down the hall. The girl's unfocused eyes meet mine, and she smiles… just before she pukes down my chest and arm… and phone.

Rux's meaty hand flies to his mouth, and the chain reaction is on.

---

*Julia*

"You okay?" Cammy presses through my headphones as I zip around the kitchen. I pull orange juice, yogurt, and a pint of fresh berries from the fridge.

"Actually, I think I am." It's probably not true, but I'm too numb to be sure, so I'm going with what I wish was the case.

"God, I can't stop looking." She's talking about the pictures of Greg that started showing up at about two this morning.

Pictures of Greg at a party with most of his team and what looks like every female fan from the Chicago area in attendance.

Greg and the little blonde with her Ace-bandage-size skirt and her hands on his chest… and *his hands* on her waist.

Greg with his big back to the camera, the little blonde's arms around his neck as he gives her a princess-style carry down some hall.

Greg with his shirt off, the little blonde mostly hidden behind him, but shown enough to see them leaning against the wall as she clutches the side of his jeans.

I swallow hard, forcing back what I can only assume is an emotional response. I'm not ready for it.

Cammy sighs. "Did you sleep at all?"

"You'd think I wouldn't, right? At first, I couldn't sleep." I was so upset about not hearing from Greg, so worried about the fact that he hadn't called. "But then I got online and, lo and behold, I found this. I gave Greg a half-hour to call and explain that even though he was wearing the exact same clothes he'd had on when he was here earlier, these pictures were actually from a year ago. Or that somehow they'd been photoshopped, and he was standing there talking to a cactus. But he never called. So I turned off my phone, and when my head hit the pillow, I was out like a blown fuse."

"That's good, I guess." After a breath, she whispers, "Have you seen the segment?"

I nod. "It's going to be fine."

It will.

Another push at my throat, but I fight it back, refusing to think about the four-million-plus viewers tuned in to what will inevitably go down as one of the greatest humiliations in network history. No. I'm not going to think about it. And with my phone still on Do Not Disturb, I've probably got at least another hour before my boss sends Agnes over here for damage control.

I take a bite of my breakfast and can't even taste it. Looking at the pint of organic berries I'd all but drooled over when I bought them, I feel the burn of tears in the back of my throat, working up my nose, and then leaking from my eyes. The dam bursts. Every part of me feels broken, and I can barely breathe through the pain.

"Aww, Julia, no. Don't cry."

"H-he r-ruined my breakfast."

She sighs. "I know he did. Asshole."

What was I thinking, letting him in the way I did?

---

*Greg*

"Dude! Greg, get up, man!"

Prying my eyes open, I turn to glare at the door Rux is barking at me through. Flashes from the night before start ping-ponging around my head, and I blow a slow calming breath through my nose.

"Greg!"

"I'm up, dickhead," I growl, swinging my legs out of his guest bed. I'm wearing a pair of his sweats and not one fucking thing more, thanks to Angela hurling all over me.

The nightstand is empty, and I feel around for my phone before remembering it too was a casualty of what smelled like half a bottle of SoCo. Right, and now I see the bag of brown rice on the floor with my phone in it.

I should have called Julia. In the light of day, a call when I was a little drunk seems like the lesser evil to not calling at all, especially considering the way the night actually played out.

"What?" I yank the door open, but the look on Rux's face is every kind of freaked out. "Shit. What's wrong? Is Angela okay? Vsev and Miser were going to make sure she got home—"

"She's fine. But uhh, Baxter, you been online at all this morning?"

Lead lands in my gut, because for Rux to be looking at me like he is, whatever it is… it's bad.

"What?"

He starts to hand me his phone but at the last second tries to pull it back. Not in the mood, I grab it anyway.

The air leaves my lungs in a punch as my eyes move from the headline "Slayers center Greg Baxter stepping out on NFL reporter Julia Wesley" to the sequence of pictures I can't make sense of. Because I know what happened, and this sure as shit doesn't look like Angela all but passing out in the hall, me carrying her to the bathroom while we were both dripping with chunks of her dinner, and then me trying to get a hold of her when she kept slipping out of my puke-slicked arms so her girlfriend could get her cleaned up enough to put her in a car.

But then I'm looking at the headline again.

"No way I said something about Julia. I wasn't that fucked up."

My eyes narrow on Rux, but he takes a step back, shaking his head.

"Not me, man." His hands wring together, and he looks like he wants to be anywhere other than where he is. "But, umm, there's something else."

Next thing, I'm watching a clip from one of those morning shows. Julia walks in to a kitchen set and greets the hosts, who are wearing aprons and pouring coffees in what must have been a prerecorded segment. My heart pounds harder seeing her, partly because that's just what happens, and partly because the look on Rux's face is warning me this isn't good.

The hosts tell her they hope she doesn't mind that they've invited another friend as well. I'm pretty sure I mind, because good money says it's Mike Rylan. They walk through to another part of the set laid out like a sunken living room. Sure enough, Mike's getting up to greet her, his clean-cut smile stretched so wide you can practically see the gleam in his white teeth. I bet they're all real.

"It's been all over social media, man. I think it aired this morning a couple hours after those pictures went up."

On the screen, Rylan goes in for a hug that shouldn't make me jealous but does.

Turning from Mike back to the hosts, Julia gives them a sly look. "What's this about, you guys?"

The hosts exchange a conspiratorial look and then spring it on her. They think she and Mike would make an adorable couple and want to set them up on a series of dates.

I can't believe what I'm seeing. I can't believe she didn't tell me about this. Only thinking back to the shitshow that was yesterday, I guess I didn't really give her the chance.

Was she upset and looking for a little comfort, when all I had to give her was my bullshit baggage, unfounded accusations, and finally a boyfriend who takes off like a chickenshit instead of staying to make sure things were right?

Jesus, why didn't I call? Why couldn't I be the man she deserves?

Julia looks less surprised than amused, like she had an idea this was coming.

She looks at Mike and smiles. "I'm sorry, Mike. But I don't think we can be more than Xbox buddies."

Mike looks at the camera and shakes his head. If this guy isn't in on the whole thing, I'm Lady Gaga. And what's this about the Xbox?

"Can you tell me why, at least?" he asks stiffly, his eyes locked on some point off-set. Yeah, he's reading from a cue card, for sure.

Julia smiles, and I stop breathing, because it's the most genuine, gorgeous smile I've ever seen.

"Well, for one, I'm a sideline reporter and you're an NFL player, so it wouldn't be professional. But there's also my boyfriend, Greg Baxter. Maybe you know him. He's the center for the Chicago Slayers."

The hosts cover their cheeks and bug their eyes, looking out over the audience with feigned shock.

I cough out a laugh, recognizing the deeper truth. This whole thing was a setup, all right. A setup so Julia could give me exactly what I've been waiting for. Hoping for.

My chest feels like it's about to burst, and I blindly reach for my phone, needing to talk to her. But then I remember. My phone is buried in a bag of dry rice in Rux's guest bedroom... where I slept instead of at Julia's... because I'm the biggest asshole on the fucking planet.

The show is still running, and Mike is talking about what a hockey fan he is. He and Julia sit down and start playing NHL on the Xbox.

Her smile is bright and clear, and it kills me to think that it's because she filmed this clip before I lost my shit over *nothing*.

Because that's what it feels like now.

She trusted me with her public image, which means she trusted me with her career. And within hours, there are pictures of me that blow the whole thing up in her face.

Shit.

Rux clears his throat. "They're actually really

good." He's talking about Julia and Mike. "And, uhh, it's pretty funny to listen to them calling the game."

Yeah, I've heard her do it before, and she's really good no matter what sport she's watching. But right now, I'm more focused on punching in her number on Rux's phone.

Waiting for a ring that doesn't come.

Straight to voicemail.

Shit.

"Clothes," I say, my panic on the rise as I grab his shoulder and haul him toward his room. "I need to borrow some clothes."

Twenty minutes later I'm at Julia's. Parking is shit, and the closest spot I can get is three blocks away. I've called half a dozen times since leaving Rux's place. I try again as I slam my car door and jog up the street.

Voicemail.

"Julia, I'll be at your place in less than five minutes. Please, you've got to believe me, it isn't what it looked like. Let me explain."

The irony of those words isn't lost on me.

I shove my hand through my hair, noticing the looks I'm getting from the pedestrians. Some have their phones out, no doubt catching a quick snap or video but I can't worry about that. I clutch Rux's phone tighter. "Let me apologize."

I hang up and pick up my pace as the dread in my gut grows.

In the lobby, I'm not even at the front desk when

the security guy who let me up yesterday blanches and takes a step back.

"Sorry, Mr. Baxter. I've been instructed not to let you up."

I stop where I am and shake my head like maybe I've got it jumbled up. But when I look back, the guy's got his hand on a phone, like he's thinking about calling the cops on it.

"Wait, look, man. Can you please call her? I swear, I'm not going to cause any trouble. But I need you to call her. Ask her if I can have five minutes. Two. I don't even need to go up. She could come down here."

"Mr. Baxter, she specifically told me you weren't welcome."

"Please. One call. Then I'll go. I'm begging."

The guy's jaw shifts and, after a breath, he reaches for the phone and pushes a button on the console.

"Ms. Wesley, it's Ronnie from the desk. I'm sorry to bother you, but Mr. Baxter is asking if—"

His yellowed eyes shift to mine, and my heart sinks. Fuck.

The door to the sidewalk opens behind me and, along with the street traffic, I catch the sound of a gathering crowd. My name bounces around along with Julia's and… Mike Rylan's?

I crank my head around and am met with a glacial stare as Mike stalks in behind me.

"What the fuck are you doing here?" I demand, like I have any right to know.

He looks me over, disgust in his eyes. "Still in town from yesterday. I'm here to check on Julia, asshole." He shakes his head and blows out a hot breath. "You have any idea how sick you make me? A girl like that? She gave you the shot *no one* gets. And this is how you treat her?"

Ronnie clears his throat from behind me, and my teeth grind down.

"Mr. Baxter, I'm afraid I have to ask you to leave. Mr. Rylan, you're welcome to take the elevators on the right."

Mike flashes a smile. "I'll head up in a minute. As soon as Baxter takes off." His arms cross over his chest, and his chin juts my way. "Unless you think something else is going to happen here?"

This is too much. This pussy football player isn't seriously thinking we're going to throw down.

"I'm not about to take a fucking swing at you, Rylan," I growl, trying to figure out how the hell I'm going to be able to get Julia to talk to me. But then the guy is back in my face.

"Why not, because of the cameras? Wouldn't think that would stop you."

I shoot a look behind me, and sure enough, the glass wall is filled with people holding their phones up, probably live-streaming this shit.

They don't matter to me, but they will to Julia. And even if they didn't, I wouldn't lay a hand on this guy, who looks like he's just waiting for an excuse to put a fist into me.

"The cameras don't mean jack," I grit out, "but Julia fucking likes you. And you caring enough about her to go toe-to-toe with me—" especially when he's got to know he'd lose, "—says maybe you're not so bad."

The fight-ready set of his jaw relaxes, and he closes his eyes.

I look toward the elevator I won't be using and then back to Mike.

Shit.

"Look, you're a pro. You've got to know not everything that gets reported is real. I'm telling you, nothing happened with that girl except she puked all over me. And when I tried to help her out, some shithead decided to make it look like something else."

Mike's got to know what I'm saying is possible, so I lay my ego down. "Please, man. Maybe she'll listen to you. Can you at least suggest there might be another explanation? Ask her to talk to me."

He runs a hand over his jaw, like he's considering it, when a sharp voice sounds from behind me.

"Greg."

Jesus, she looks as pissed as she sounds, but I've never seen or heard anything better in my life. I'll be able to explain. To make this right.

"Julia, thank God."

I start toward her, but her hand comes up to stop me.

"No. Greg, we're done. I don't want to talk to you. I don't want to see you or hear about you trying to get to me through the people I care about." She looks past me to the growing wall of observers beyond the glass. "If you have even a shred of respect for me or my career, you'll leave without making any more of a scene."

Her words hit worse than any blow. She's cutting me off.

If I go now, we're done. For as many years as I've known her, one thing about Julia has never changed. When it comes to guys, she doesn't give second chances. But she looks like she's hanging on by a thread, and I can't even imagine how she's going to stand up from under the damage I've already caused. If I stay, it'll be even worse.

A hand lands on my shoulder, and I turn to Mike, who's nodding toward Ronnie. "There a back way out of here? A rear exit he can use?"

I want to dig in my heels and shake off Mike's hold. I want to take Julia in my arms and beg her to listen. But I owe her more than that. So I go.

## Chapter 20

*Greg*

*P*RACTICE IS ROUGH. The guys give me a wide berth on the ice and off. Everyone's heard about the morning show segment and seen the pictures. Everyone except Vsev, who is dumb enough to miss practice and isn't answering his phone.

I cut up and down the ice, firing pucks one after another, going hard on the drills, even though my focus is shit. The minute I step off the ice, Coach pulls me aside to chew my ass out about staying sharp no matter what goes down in my personal life and tell me to get my head right for tomorrow's game.

I know it's what I need to do, but all I can see is Julia's face as I walked out on her.

It's her voice I hear when we board the plane that night for Vegas, and it's her red-rimmed eyes from when I showed up at her building that haunt me when I try to sleep.

She's on my mind the next day when we get to the rink for the game, but for one hot minute when I push into the locker room, that changes.

"Fucking married?" Rux barks, eyes wide, chin pulled back.

Vsev is wearing a smug smile, turning in a slow circle as he holds up his left hand for everyone to see the enormous gold band studded with diamonds on his fourth finger.

"Wait, you were here?" I ask, dropping my shit and walking up to my youngest teammate, ready to shake some sense into him. "You have any idea what this stunt could cost you?"

The nod I get back is confident and sure. "I sit this game. Coach very angry when I call, but he understand."

Everyone groans, and Vsev pats the air in front of him to settle them.

"I have wife now. We celebrate after game."

I'm almost afraid to ask. "Dude, how did you meet this girl? Do you know anything about her?"

He laughs like I'm the funniest guy he's ever met and claps me on the shoulder. "You introduce us! My wife is Angela. I take her home after the party and she ask me to stay."

Apparently, they spent the night talking, and by morning, the kid was booking a flight to Vegas.

Vsev waves me closer, his expression turning somber. "I hear what happen with your Julia." He shakes his head. "I know girl who put pictures out. I get her to give me all photos this morning. You have them after game."

I stand there and gape. "What? How?"

Nodding to the side, he rubs a hand over the patchy stubble on his jaw. "She is girl I spend time with before I take Angela home. She get jealous and want my Angela to look bad, but I know better."

I pull the guy in for a hug, my eyes dangerously close to watering. "Thank you, man. And congratulations. But any chance I can get those files now? I need to send them to a friend."

When we take the ice, I'm pumped, jacked up and playing like Julia might be watching. We win six to two, three of those points being mine. After the game, everyone wants a piece of me. They want a statement on my relationship with Julia, they want to know who the girl in the photos was, and they want to know how I was able to play a game like that with everything else that's going on. I don't have time for any of it and cut through the crowd, dripping wet with sweat. Wearing my skates and gear, I find a spot at the back of the locker room to call. I'm praying something's changed in the hours since I forwarded the files and she'll pick up. That I'll at least hear the phone ring more than once and know she unblocked me.

No dice.

The adrenaline that's been pumping hot through my veins starts to cool, and I check my messages.

**Mike: Showed her the pictures. She believes nothing happened, but she still doesn't want to see you. Sorry, man.**

---

*Julia*

"Julia, did you hear me?" my new agent, Midge McCalister, nudges from across the desk in her Chicago office three days later. With her sharp eyes, neat black bob, and immaculate power suit, she's the epitome of controlled—despite the recent developments we've yet to spin into anything but the train wreck they are. "It's one game… okay, it's probably two. But we have no reason to believe you won't be back on the field after that."

I've heard it before.

They want to let the dust settle on the media feeding frenzy. Wait until people stop digging up and dissecting every photo taken of Greg and me together since sophomore year of high school.

For now, I'm doing the behind-the-scenes work. Making sure Jane Josnick is up and running while she fills in.

"I know you said you weren't interested, but before I officially decline… there are two dating show offers. One to host, one as a participant—"

I hold up my hand to stop her. "I'm sure. That's not the direction I want my career to go. Even if I'm delegated to behind-the-scenes work, sports is where my heart is."

"Got it." Setting the two files aside, she crosses her arms over her desk and meets my eyes. "This will blow over, Julia. Just give it some time."

I swallow thickly. "Plenty of that."

After the meeting I take a cab back to my apartment and, kneeling when I get in the door, soak up Matty's tight hug.

"Mommy says you need a big one," he gasps, using all his might to squeeze me.

Laughing, I stand, bringing him up with me. Cammy's walking toward the washer with a basket of clothes, tenderness in her eyes as she watches her little boy comfort me. In the next blink he's had enough and squirms free to dart off to the living room where he's been hanging ornaments on our artificial tree.

"You didn't have to cut your trip short." I take the basket from her hands, and we walk back to the laundry nook.

She shrugs, propping a hip against the machine as she piles Spider-Man T-shirts and Hulk briefs into the machine. "You didn't have to drop everything to take me in when Jeremy decided he'd rather join the military and be stationed overseas than stick around and help me raise our son."

The air in my lungs feels heavy, like all the sighs in the world won't be enough to ease them. "It's not the same thing."

"Isn't it? The man you trusted to be there with you jumping ship the second things don't go exactly the way he's comfortable with?" She shakes her head. "I shouldn't have pushed you with him. But I thought— it's *Greg*. He's different. He has to be."

She starts the machine, and we head back to the living room, where I slide off my heels and tuck my feet beneath me on the couch.

"I think that's my biggest problem. I know he wasn't unfaithful. He didn't hook up with the girl at that party, and even if I hadn't seen the real pictures, I think I would have believed him on that. But… I *trusted* him." My voice cracks, and I meet my sister's under-standing eyes. "I mean, can you even imagine if I'd actually been pregnant?" If somehow, our birth control failed and we'd created a miraculous little life between us… and he'd just taken off. Like my father. And Cammy's father. And fucking Jeremy, who couldn't be there for my sister but then two years later married some German girl.

I'm not ready for a baby. It's not part of my plan for at least another three years. But with Greg, I thought if something like that did happen, I could count on him to be there to face it with me. I'd finally let myself believe he wasn't the kind of guy who would leave.

Cammy scoots close and wraps her arms around my shoulders. "I'm so sorry."

I nod.

"Me too."

---

*Greg*

THEY FUCKING cut her from the game.

I want to puke, and then I want to punch someone, but my game against the Flyers just ended, taking all opportunities for venting some aggression with it.

"Baxter, quite a game tonight. That fight in the first get into your head at all?"

There's a mic aimed at me and someone with a job much like Julia's on the other end of it. I think of her and force myself to give a straight answer, to keep my temper in check. To remember, we're all just doing our jobs.

Then I go back to my stall and dump my gear. I shower and pass on the guys' invitation to go out. When I get back to the apartment that hasn't felt right since Julia stopped sleeping in it with me, I send her another text she won't read. And wait for the call that won't come.

I'm doing the same thing a few nights later when

there's a knock on my door. My heart starts to slam, because with the security in this building, there aren't a lot of people who have access to my front door. But Julia? She's one of them.

I throw on some jeans and whip a T-shirt over my head as I tear down the hall, all the things I need her to hear rushing through my head.

Apology poised on my tongue, I jerk open the door and—

"You never call… you never write." Dressed in jeans and a cashmere coat, Jack Hastings flashes a dry smile.

*Not Julia.*

It feels like I ran into a brick wall head-on. And then it fucking landed on me.

"Jack." I lean into the jamb of the door, letting it hold me up. "What are you doing here?"

He holds up a six-pack of craft beer, two of which have been replaced with the light beer I usually drink.

"Wagner's bringing a pizza." His hand comes up between us and he narrows his eyes. "I don't want one fucking word about not being up for it, because I essentially had to move heaven and earth to get him to come out and give Abby a night off from his unrelenting adoration. So all I want from you is a little gratitude, got it?"

I weigh my options. Jack's fit. Probably six feet. Works out. But I'm bigger—hell, I'm bigger than most everyone. Him though, I've got beat by five inches and fifty pounds of muscle. Which means if I want him out, he's going.

Thing is, he owns this building. And if he wants me out, I go.

Not that he'd do anything like that. We go back to high school, and on any given day when my heart isn't fucking torn up like this, we get on good. But today?

He doesn't wait for my okay, instead shouldering past me into the apartment with his mismatched beer and good intentions.

The elevator dings before I can close the door, and then I've got Hank pushing into my space too. But at least he's got a Lou Malnati's in hand.

We park it in the living room, Jack sinking into the spot on the couch where Julia sometimes researched the teams she'd be covering that week. I loved the look of her pale legs against the charcoal leather and how she took up even more space than I did when she had all her stuff spread out around her.

Jack clears his throat. "Dude, mind turning your broken-heart high beams on Hank a minute so I can eat?"

Jesus.

I wipe a hand over my face and pull it together.

Hank bites off half his slice and follows it with a long swig of beer. Giving his glasses a shove up his nose, he cuts to the chase. "What are you doing to get her back?"

"Yeah, because every time you blow out onto the

ice since all this went down with Julia, it's like the entire arena shivers, wondering if this is the night you lose your shit. And seriously, seeing that mopey mug of yours after each game is depressing the hell out of me." Leave it to Jack to pass off his concern as something self-serving. He acts like he's got a heart made of Teflon, but deep, deep, *deep* down, the guy can't stand to see shit that needs fixing, people who are hurting… and not try to do something about it.

I cut a look at Hank, who gives me a slight shake of his head and an eye roll. "Jack's exaggerating."

"The hell I am." Pointing a folded slice at Hank, he adds, "You fucking told me yourself, Abby was almost crying when she saw him in the post-game."

Hank shoves in another bite big enough to have me wondering if I should do a quick search for Heimlich techniques. Guess we're leaving it at that.

I sit forward, elbows on my knees, beer hanging between my hands. "I don't know what to do. I fucked up."

Ten minutes later, they have the broad strokes of what happened and a few of the finer points. People say talking about shit is healing, but all I feel is raw from reliving the mistake that cost me the only thing that matters.

"I've called a hundred times to apologize. Emailed to explain what was going through my head. But she's blocked my calls, and I can only imagine she's handling the rest the same way. I want to go over there, but they've already pulled her off two games because of the bad press with this situation. The last thing I want to do is make it worse."

Jack whistles through his teeth and shakes his head like the situation I've presented him with is every bit as futile as it feels. "What we need is to get you a *distraction*. Someone to take your mind off—"

"Nope," Hank cuts in, giving Jack an exasperated look. "Don't listen to him. Distractions aren't going to get you any closer to where you want to be."

Pretty sure Jack's talking about another woman, and I'm grateful to Hank for having some sense. The idea of being with anyone but Julia makes me almost as sick as thinking of her with anyone but me.

Grabbing another piece of pizza, Hank folds it over and eyes it, considering. "She's more about football than hockey, right?"

Not exactly the reminder I need right then, but— "Yeah, why?"

When his eyes come up, they're as serious as I've ever seen them. "Then maybe you ought to start thinking like a football player."

I stare at him and then look to Jack, whose WTF face matches my thinking.

*Football?* I grab the box of pizza and point to the door. "Get out."

## Chapter 21

*Julia*

IT'S ONE OF those moody December days where it's still too warm to snow and the cloud cover is low enough it hides the tops of the buildings. There's a gray wash to the city and a damp chill in the air as my cab cuts through downtown. But I could be buried under every blanket I own, and I'd still feel cold.

It's been almost two weeks, and all I can think about is Greg. How, for ten years, he would have been the very first person I would call to talk about what was going on with my career. How, even before we were together, he filled a place in my life where no one else quite fit.

I miss him.

I miss the friendship I so fiercely protected all those

years ago, and I miss the relationship that made me feel whole in a way I've never felt before.

Every day I want to call him, pretend that nothing's changed and the past two weeks didn't happen. But then I remember the way he looked leaving. How I felt sitting there waiting for him to come back.

So stupid.

Like the worst fool.

More alone than I'd ever been.

And so, every day I put the phone down before I do something I'll regret. I focus on taking the tarnish off my reputation and being ready for getting back on the field… for about ten minutes, until I'm eyeing my phone again.

There's another new message this morning.

Cammy thinks I ought to delete them all. Clear him out completely. But I can't quite make myself do it.

My thumb hovers over the voicemail icon.

I promised I wouldn't listen, but maybe just one. Just to hear his voice. Maybe it won't affect me the way it used to.

Heart racing, I play a message from earlier in the week.

"Hey beautiful," he begins with that low rumbling voice that touches every tender part of me. This is a mistake. "Coach's coffeemaker blew up before practice this morning. I didn't even know those little single cup machines could do that, but the guy came tearing out of his office like a fucking bear on fire. Little bits of grounds splattered all over his shirt, MFs flying out of his mouth left and right. Obviously, he's fine. I know you'll worry about that. But after the way he's been riding my ass about my attitude—not gonna lie, it was about the funniest damn thing I've seen in a long time." There's a smile in his tone, but I hear it fade with his sigh. "I know you aren't listening. I know it's stupid to keep leaving you messages you won't ever hear. But I can't help it. I miss talking to you. I miss your smile and your laugh. So like the total wuss I am, I'm calling your voicemail every day to hear your outgoing message and then talking like you're still listening. Like you're still my girl. Like I haven't lost—fuck." The word grates out rough and so pained, my throat clogs and I have to blink back tears. Then quietly, like he's no longer talking to me, he says, "I've lost everything."

There's silence, and I think maybe he's going to hang up. I think it's the end, and my heart feels like it's breaking all over again. Like I can't bear it. But then his throat clears, and he's back. "Anyway, I hope you're having a better day than Coach. I love you, Jules. Talk to you tomorrow."

The cab pulls to a stop in front of my building, and I quickly wipe at my tear-streaked cheeks. I shouldn't have listened.

Because now I want to hear the rest.

The cabby cranks around in his seat, giving me a dead-eyed stare. Right. Time to get out.

I head inside the bleached stone mammoth that

houses our offices, aching over Greg's message. Why is he still calling?

The guys at the security desk wave, and a friend calls my name from across the lobby.

Why did Greg have to sound so much like I feel?

I reply to a text from Midge, confirming I can meet with her this afternoon.

Then I count the messages Greg has left me since that awful night, wondering if he sounds like that in all of them.

Why is he still fighting for me… when he *walked away*?

The elevator doors are sliding closed when one last passenger cuts between them.

Ugh. Ray.

"Julie! Glad I caught you. This saves me a call." His mouth pulls down at the corners. "We need to talk."

My skin prickles. I don't want to talk with Ray right now, but I won't say no. How can I, when the decision on next week's game will be made tonight?

Bracing myself, I follow him back to his office and close the door behind me.

"It's close, Julie. Too close."

My heart sinks. "They aren't sure about next week?"

He lets out a slow breath and waves me toward the seating area in his office. There are boxes and files on all the chairs, leaving only the couch. "Sit. I'll tell you what I know."

I close my eyes. *Not today*.

"I'm too antsy to sit, Ray. What's going on?"

"They're still not convinced the situation is stable enough. That viewers will believe you're grounded, settled. That your judgment can be trusted." His expression is a mask of sympathy, but I've known this man long enough to recognize the calculation in his eyes. "I can help you."

My arms cross, and I take a step back. I don't like the sound of this. "Help me how, Ray?"

"Be with me, Julie. You need my protection, now more than ever. Have dinner with me tonight." He steps into the space I just put between us, and dropping his voice, says, "Honey, no one would dare to make a move against you if we were *together*."

Together.

I swallow past the hot rise of nausea resulting from his offer. I've had enough.

I make myself smile politely at Ray, because I'm a professional, even if he isn't. "I'm going to pass on your offer. It's not appropriate. And if the key to my career is tied to who I date instead of the kind of reporting I do —well, then I'm not interested. Thing is, I'm fairly confident, it's not." I open the door and glance back. "And Ray, don't call me honey. My name is *Julia*."

I haven't felt much more than the ache in my chest since everything fell apart with Greg. But right now, I feel free. I feel proud.

And I feel like there's only one person on the planet

I want to call and tell.

Instead, I walk over to reception and book the small conference room for the afternoon. It's barely bigger than my cube, with bland beige walls and a utilitarian table with two serviceable chairs. Nothing fancy, but more than enough for what I need to do.

I sit down and cue up the first message. It's a pleading free flow of panicked apologies for leaving the way he did and urgent explanations about what *didn't* happen at that party. It's heartbreaking, because if I'd heard that message twelve hours before he actually sent it, maybe we wouldn't be where we are.

My stomach hurts thinking that.

Greg panicked and took off, yes. But he wasn't the only one to run.

But he *was* the only one who kept coming back.

I force myself to keep listening. To hear every word he said to me. It's painful, but it's important.

The message playing must have been from about a week after we broke up.

He's sorry. He misses me. He loves me. But there's more.

"I never told you about Shelly." He sounds tired, and I see the time stamp was near two a.m. "It's not a question, like, 'Did I tell you?' I didn't. But I should have. It wouldn't make my actions any less shitty, but at least maybe you wouldn't have had so many questions about why."

He tells me about the woman he'd thought he

loved, and how she'd been trying to scam her way into a lifetime of child support. How hard it had been waiting to find out if he was a father. And how it had been even harder coming to terms with the fact that she'd been playing him from the start. That nothing about what he'd thought they had or how she'd felt about him had been real.

It had gone on for months and months, nearly costing him the career he'd sacrificed everything for. There hadn't been a baby, and it had taken him some time to figure out how he felt about that.

My heart hurts knowing that he'd had to go through all of that. That anyone could betray him that way is sickening.

"This probably sounds like making excuses, and you feel like you won't be able to trust me not to take off on you again. But Julia, you have to understand. Until a week ago, nothing in my life has terrified me like what happened with that woman. But now I know what real fear is. It's losing you."

When I'm able to see past the tears, I read through all the texts and open all the emails. I'd thought the first messages were going to be the hardest. I was wrong. The last ones cut the worst. The ones where Greg sounds resigned to what we had being over… but still hasn't been able to let go.

It's been hours, and I've gone through my entire pouch of travel tissues crying, trying to figure out how to make this right. The Slayers play the Bruins tomorrow night. Which means Greg's probably halfway to Boston already.

I could call him. But ambushing him when he's surrounded by his teammates with no way to get away hardly seems fair.

There's only the message from this morning left to play, and as it begins, I start pulling up flights to Boston.

"Julia. This is it. No more calls. So, if I don't talk to you again… know that I mean it when I say I wish you the very best in life."

The air stops moving through my lungs, and my phone clatters to the table.

Oh God. He's letting me go.

Stumbling out of my chair, I sweep my phone and laptop into my oversized bag. My feet can't move quickly enough as I cut through the halls to the elevator. I'm halfway through the lobby when I hear the sharp sound of my name and swing around to find my boss, red-faced and huffing after me.

"Bill, I'm sorry, I'm on my way out." Whatever decision they make about me covering the game, I'll hear about tomorrow morning.

"Whoa, slow down a second. I wasn't expecting you in today, or I would have hunted you down earlier. You doing okay?"

Chances are good that I look like hell, but it's the last thing I'm worried about. "I'm fine. I only came in to pull tapes for next week's games, but I got side-tracked."

His head snaps forward, eyes sharp. "Tell me this means you're up for this week's game. We're coming up on playoffs, and I need my best. Jane doesn't gel with the game producers the way you do. Honestly, there was some action on the field you would have been on top of that she flat-out missed. I've been putting off announcing who was going to cover, hoping you'd be back." He winces and grinds his teeth before grudgingly adding, "But if you need more time, I'll give that Bradley kid a shot."

If *I* need more time? What the hell?

"Bill, I'm absolutely ready for the game. I've already done the prep. Thing is, I really need to get to the airport, so I can't talk to you about this now. I'll be back in time to fly out with everyone for the pregame prep, but before then, I'll have to talk to you by phone or email."

The color washes from his face. "Interview?"

"What? No. It's personal." I stop and shake my head. I'm through living a half life and pretending the things that matter to me aren't important. It's better Bill knows what's going on, and he can decide how to handle it from there. "I'm going to Boston to see Greg Baxter."

He lets out a relieved gust of breath. "Look, I'm all for you kids working it out. But I need you here in Chicago for the next three hours. After that, I'll pop for the flight to Boston myself. First-class."

That's it?

I'm still trying to get over my shock about his nonchalance regarding an athlete relationship when the rest registers. Bill's notoriously cheap, so him covering my flight means whatever this is, it's big. "What's going on?"

Eyes cutting around the lobby, he drops his voice. "Rylan. He's got an announcement. I'm thinking it's the shoulder. You were the first one to pick up on it, so you earned the spot. But more importantly, he asked for you specifically. He's offering an exclusive."

If it were anyone other than Mike.

"Two hours."

Bill claps his hands once and nods, grinning at me. "Going to be good having you back, Wesley. No one knows the game like you."

I nod and then— "Hey Bill, what gave you the idea I wasn't up for the games?"

"Hmm? Hettler. Said you were having a tough time. Needed a break." Brows furrowing, he asks, "That not accurate?"

My blood boils, but I hold it together, keeping my voice level and calm when I respond. "How about in the future we leave Ray out of the loop when it comes to calls about my career?"

Bill's eyes go deadly sharp. "Done." Next thing I know his phone is at his ear, and he's walking back toward the elevator. "Agnes, set up whatever travel Julia Wesley needs tonight, and get HR in my office ASAP… Yeah, Ray Hettler."

## Chapter 22

*Julia*

ℕINETY MINUTES LATER, I'm seated across from Mike Rylan in the private room of a popular Lakeview bar, wrapping things up. I know Mike was only trying to help by calling on me specifically to cover this, and it means a lot. And I'm glad for him that he isn't announcing his retirement… but still, Mike's off-season plans to host a dating show hardly merit my delay. I need to get to Boston and talk to Greg.

I unclip my mic and hand it off to a PA who waves goodbye while the rest of the small crew carries out the gear.

"Congratulations again, Mike. The show sounds great," I say, grabbing my coat and purse from the booth behind us. I didn't have time to pack a bag, but all I need is my wallet to get on a plane.

To get to Greg. Please, don't let me be too late.

Mike shoves his hands into his pockets and looks around the now-empty room. "Yeah, well, it's the start of a necessary transition. I've got one more season in me, but after that?"

What he's telling me wasn't part of the interview, and I turn back. "I wondered."

"I know. And hell, when the time is right… maybe the exclusive for that announcement will get me back in your good graces."

I give him a questioning look, and that aww-shucks smile quirks as he shrugs, backing away. "Don't hate me, Julia."

Hate him?

Only then, I feel it, this sort of warm and tingly sense of awareness washing over me. I freeze, my lungs locked around my next breath.

"*Jules.*"

Slowly, I turn, emotion clogging my throat as I take in my first look at the man I haven't seen in weeks but haven't been able to get out of my mind for a minute. He's dressed in a dark suit, his hair is a sexy dark mess, and his too-blue eyes are fixed on me with an intensity that pins me to my spot.

Distantly, I register Mike giving my shoulder a pat as he walks away, but I'm too shocked, too absorbed by the man standing in front of me to reply.

Greg's nostrils flare, and the muscles in his hard-cut jaw flex as he brushes a knuckle against my cheek.

I feel it then.

A lone tear, wetting my skin as he wipes it away.

"Tears?" he asks, but the word is hoarse, like it wounds him.

I say the only thing my sluggish brain can think of. "You're supposed to be in Boston." Oh God, why isn't he there? I look him over in a panic. "Are you injured? Are you hurt?"

"No." The corner of his mouth hitches up, but that barely-there smile doesn't meet his eyes. "Keeping track of me, Jules?"

More tears push past my lids. I can't believe he's here.

"Jesus, I'm sorry. I didn't want to make you cry." Thick fingers plow through his hair as he mutters, "Great fucking plan, Baxter."

I see what my tears do to him and brush them away. I want to fling myself into his arms and tell him I'm sorry, that I love him—but after that last message telling me no more calls, I'm not sure I still have the right. "I'm fine. Emotional. So… this is a plan?"

"A shitty one, from the looks of it." He wipes a hand over his face. "I just wanted to talk to you. Once." He swallows, searching my eyes. "And don't worry. This isn't going to blow up all over social media. Anyone with a phone is going to have it aimed out front where Jack, Hank and Mike are playing darts."

"*Jack*?"

"Yeah, I know." He shakes his head like it's better I don't ask, then waves a hand to the swinging door behind us. "The guy who owns Belfast here, Brody, said we could use his office to talk. Will you give me a minute?"

Praying we have more than that, I follow him through the kitchen and around to an office with a large black couch and an oversized desk and chair. He locks the door behind us and for a moment just stands there, one arm braced against the solid wood above his head, the neat lines of his suit underscoring the powerful build beneath.

"Greg?" I say it softly, tentatively reaching for his shoulder, only to pull back at the last second.

His head drops forward. "I thought maybe if I could talk to you again… maybe we could find our way back to something where I could hear your laugh once in a while. See your smile. Because I fucking miss it, Julia."

"I miss you too." So much. I've missed my friend. The one with the strict limit on what we were to each for more than a decade. And even more, the one he's become these last months.

"How have you been?" he asks, turning so he's standing with his back against the door, arms crossed over his broad chest.

I laugh at the casual question, but even I can hear the heartbreak in it. "I've been better. You?"

"I'm not sleeping great. Been spending more time with my sister these last two weeks. Less with the team outside of practices. I love those guys, but they can be a bunch of meatheads."

"How's Natalie?" I ask, but I'm thinking those meatheads are his best friends. I can't imagine him wanting to avoid them, except I haven't exactly been sticking to my usual routine either. I've switched some of the classes I take at the gym for more solitary work-outs on the treadmill and rowing machine. I've been passing on lunches and dinner plans. Avoiding the situations where the people who know me best would have the opportunity to see that I'm not myself. To try to cheer me up when it feels like I'm dying inside.

It feels like that now.

I'm physically aching to touch him, to bury my head against his chest. Soak in the woodsy scent of him and the warmth I haven't felt since we said goodbye.

Since *I* said goodbye.

"Nat? Same as always," he says. "Sweet. Annoying. Well-intentioned and misguided." His eyes crinkle at the edges. "She made me zucchini bread with protein powder to cheer me up."

"Cammy made me a batch of chocolate chip cookie dough to eat raw."

"Damn. That sounds way better. Think we can work out some kind of little sister exchange for a week or two?"

I laugh, really laugh at the envy in his voice, and

when Greg smiles, it's like something inside my chest opens, letting in the first fresh air and sunshine it's seen in weeks.

He watches me until my laughter dies and we're standing in this borrowed space, eyes locked across a divide neither of us seems to know how to breach.

"That laugh, it's what I came for," he says, the ghost of his smile all that's left on his lips. "What I needed."

He takes a deep breath, his brows furrow, and his eyes move over me in a slow crawl. I can see the debate in them when they stop at my mouth, feel that pull tugging between us. But then that look is gone. One of resignation in its place.

He clears his throat, eyes lingering on me a few seconds before breaking contact. "Maybe you wouldn't mind if I texted you sometime?"

He's offering friendship. A safe way to keep him in my life without having to risk anything. It kills me.

For two weeks I've been telling myself I never should have let Greg so close. That I should have known better than to allow myself to become so vulnerable. And for two weeks, I haven't been able to shake this ever-growing sense of *wrong*. The persistent whisper in my head warning that I was making a mistake.

But in this moment, standing so close to him… I know with a soul-deep certainty that kind of safety would break my heart.

"Greg," I whisper, shaking my head as I cross the

divide to stand in front of him. My hands catch the sides of his suit. His eyes follow the motion, moving from one hand to the other before slowly coming up to meet mine. "I miss you. So much."

Brushing a few strands of hair from my brow, he lets out a shaky breath. "So that's a yes to the texts? To maybe seeing if we can find our way back to being in each other's lives again? As friends."

Friends. "Is that all you want?"

"What I want is—" He cuts off the gruff words, but I see the admission in his eyes before he closes them.

My heart beats faster, stronger.

Cupping the side of his beautiful face, I brush his heavy cheekbone, taking solace in the sound of his low groan.

Can he feel my hand shaking or sense how scared I am?

"I miss *us*."

Those bright blue eyes pop open, meeting mine with a stare so intense I lose my breath beneath it, can barely whisper my next words. "I miss the conversations that stretch from one day into the next and laughing until my stomach hurts. I miss your arms around me and that feeling of *right* I've never had with anyone else. I miss my best friend showing me day after day how much more we are to each other."

His hand covers mine, and holding it in his grip, he pulls it down to his chest, pressing it against his hard-beating heart. "Julia, what are you saying?"

"I'm saying I'm sorry. I was scared and hurt, but I shouldn't have cut you off the way I did. I told myself that you were the one who left when things got tough, but really, it was me. I thought I was protecting myself. Doing the right thing. The smart thing. But I've never been more wrong in my entire life."

Greg's breath comes out in a punch. Wrapping his hand around the back of my neck, he pulls me in and presses his brow to mine. "Christ, Julia, don't say you're sorry. I pushed and pushed for your trust, and the minute you gave it to me, I let you down." His fingers tighten. "But I swear to you, I won't do it again. Give me another chance, and I'll never give you a reason to doubt me, *us*, again."

His words make me ache. In the past I haven't been able to let go of my doubts and insecurities. But now, I *believe*.

I know this man.

I *love* this man.

He's good and loyal and honest and driven… and even though I gave him every reason to, he hasn't given up on me.

"You have it," I whisper into the space where we cling to each other.

The bridge of his nose brushes mine. "Jules, you promised me another kiss at our next reunion. What do you say to an advance?"

My heart beats harder. "I can give you that. But I'll expect to be paid back *in full*."

His breath huffs out in a laugh heavy with emotion. He tips my head, cradling it in his powerful hands. There's amusement and tenderness in his eyes, and the first real hint of that cocky smile I haven't seen in a long time hanging from his lips.

"You won't regret this."

He parts my lips with the softest brush of his own. The tender contact is light and gentle and just the beginning. Chills skate across my skin, and all those knotted nerves ease, giving way to butterflies taking flight by the dozens in my belly. My arms slide around his neck as my fingers find their way into his tousled mess of hair. Soaking in the clean, manly scent of him and the warmth of being this close, I close my eyes.

It feels like being home.

"*Julia.*"

Then he's kissing me harder, his arms locking around my back and waist. Holding me close as his tongue glides against mine. Our breath is ragged, the need between us hot and sharp.

His big hand crushes my hair. "God, I missed you."

My shoulders hit the wall, and then I have the decadent weight of Greg's big body pinning me where I stand.

*Yes.*

We can't get close enough, can't stop the rush of hands and heated, breathless words. Promises and pleas tumble between us, as urgent as our touch.

"I love you," I gasp, and he pulls back to meet my eyes. Nostrils flared, brows drawn forward, he nods.

"Good. That's going to make convincing you to marry me a lot easier."

There's no time to think or respond or shower his gorgeous face with kisses before he crushes me beneath his kiss again, growling against my mouth and neck and chest that he loves me, that he wants me, that I'm everything.

He's wrong.

*We're* everything. Together.

Slowly, painfully, Greg draws back. "We've got to stop, or I'm going to do something that will ensure Brody never lends out his office again."

He's right. "What do you say we get out of here?"

He brushes the hair from my brow and fastens the top two buttons on my blouse. "Much as I don't want to let you go, even for a second, I'll cut out the back so you leave from the front. We can keep things quiet as long as you like, Jules. We can keep them quiet forever if that's what you need."

The sincerity in his eyes touches me. He knows what he's offering—he's lived with it before—and he means it.

*This man.*

I reach for his belt and unabashedly refasten it. Yes, we've been here before, but this time it's different. "I love you."

His eyes close, and he blows out an emotional

breath. "I love you too, Jules. I'm never going to let you go."

"Promise?" I ask, taking his big hand in mine.

He nods, that cocky smile slanting at full strength. "Swear."

I press a quick kiss to his lips and pull the door open wide. "Good. Then let's go see how your friends are doing with darts while we wait on an Uber."

He's stock still beside me. Shocked silent by my suggestion, I'm guessing, but not for long. Greg Baxter is a man who has made his career thinking on his feet. One look at my smile and his is back, blinding and brilliant as he pulls me toward the front of the bar where Jack is pulling his dart from the bullseye.

The crowd parts for us, heads turning as we pass. I squeeze Greg's hand tighter, and the smile he gives me warms me through.

"Nice toss, man," Greg says, clapping Jack on the shoulder.

Jack's eyes shift between us, and his cocky grin spreads. "*No way*." Turning to Hank, he adds, "I can't fucking believe your football play worked. And to think, this jackass tried to kick us out."

"Football?" My brows shoot high, and I turn to Greg, who groans.

This I've got to hear.

"It wasn't football," he protests, giving each of his buddies a glare.

Hank shoves his geeky stud billionaire glasses up his

nose. "Quarterback sneak. Got the offensive team pushing forward, keeping everyone out of the way, while our QB ran with the ball."

Oh, this is too good. Beaming up at Greg, I whisper, "You played quarterback to get me back?"

His arm lashes around my lower back, pulling me close to his side. "I'd do anything for you. Even play quarterback."

Surrounded by a crowd, many with their phones out and undoubtedly recording, I wrap my hand around Greg's tie and slowly reel him in, closer and closer still, until his face looms inches above mine. Eyes locked, I whisper, "Brace yourself," and then, pushing up onto my toes, close that last distance to kiss him.

His hands settle on my waist, gripping once before sliding around to my back as we linger in the soft press of our lips. It's a kiss more about a promise than the passion we'll give in to once we're alone. It's sweet and tame, but when we break apart, both of us are breathless and smiling like fools.

This is the beginning of the us I won't ever try to hide.

I rest my hand over Greg's heart. "We should probably get out of here."

"Where do you want to go? I'll take you anywhere, Jules."

He would. But there's only one place I want to go. "Boston."

His head rocks back and he laughs, pulling me into a tight hug that I tighten even more.

"I'm serious, Greg. You've got a game tomorrow. We gotta go."

Tilting my head back, he presses another sweet and soulful kiss to my lips.

"You gonna wear my jersey?"

"Try to stop me."

# Epilogue

*Jack*

*I*T'S BEEN SIX months since I delivered up my latest happily ever after—not that I get any fucking credit for my efforts, thank you very much —and we're back at the bar where it all came together. Belfast is hopping, but parked at our high-top by the bar, we might as well be any other set of customers. Sure, people notice Julia, Greg, and the Wagners, and hell, sometimes me too, but aside from a nod or smile we're pretty much left to enjoy our night out. The bar's cool, with a pressed copperplate ceiling, exposed brick walls, and a chill atmosphere. It's the perfect spot to grab a drink when our schedules line up. Bonus points because those little white lights they've got strung around have the rock on Julia's finger throwing off enough strobes we ought to put a seizure warning on it.

Julia's still working as a sideline reporter, but she's got another gig now too. Her own weekly show where she invites pro athletes from various sports to play Xbox and shoot the shit about what's going on in their personal and professional lives. It's an ultra-casual format, but between that chick's sport knowledge and her easy repartee with the players, the show has turned into an instant hit. Viewers can't get enough of her trash talk and bickering over league records and player stats. And Greg can't get enough of her.

The wedding's next month, and Ruxton Meyers is going to be the best man. I get it. Baxter didn't want Hank to feel weird if he picked me. Understandable, since Wagner was the one to come up with the whole quarterback sneak thing. Sure, I mean, yeah, I'm the guy who knew which buttons to push to guilt Mr. Billionaire Brainiac into putting his thinking cap on for Greg's benefit, but whatever. I don't need the stroke. Hank, though? Hell, every time Abby pulls out that adoring look, calling him her romantic hero, the guy sits a little taller. Gives her that dopey, completely whipped, hard-crush smile he's damn lucky I'd forgotten about in the years since they dated in high school. Not sure I'd have gone to the trouble to get them back together if I had.

Joking, joking.

*Mostly.*

Straightening my tie, I sit back and admire my handiwork: two totally whipped but considerably happier dudes than they were when they moved into my building a couple years ago. I'm giving myself a well-deserved pat on the back, basking in my romantic achievements, when the front door to the bar swings open, and my self-satisfied smile falls flat.

I know that neat part and smooth fall of straight chestnut hair. I know the soft pout of that full bottom lip and the tight stitch of concentration between her arched brows.

Laurel Matthews. My buddy Law's sister.

And she's probably counting the patrons to see if she needs to file a complaint over max capacity. Or working up a mental flow chart on how to get to the empty table in the back corner.

God, she made sixth grade miserable. Ninth, even worse. And don't get me started on senior year. But now she's gone and ruined what was fast becoming my new favorite bar.

That searching, anxious stare works its way across the crowd and lands on me with a thud, the hot flash of irritation in her eyes only half of what she's got to be seeing in mine.

I toss back half my bourbon, savoring the burn as I raise a brow in greeting.

Those soft full lips form an F-bomb, and she starts searching the bar again before coming back to me.

She looks nervous, uneasy, and my attention shifts to the tool standing beside her, a smug, sort of expectant look in eyes that are just a smidge too eager for my taste.

I don't like him.

"Hey, isn't that Laurel Matthews?" Abby asks, grinning, her elbow digging into my ribs.

I'm vaguely aware of Hank choking on his beer as his head spindles around to where—shit, she's walking toward us, an inexplicable grin on her lips and the tool close on her heels.

Greg leans forward. "Uhh, how many years has it been since you guys last saw each other?"

Not enough. "Not sure. She wasn't at the reunion. Summer after freshman year, maybe."

Definitely. Much as it grates, I remember the white sundress she was wearing, the narrow straps over shoulders freckled by the sun.

What the hell is she doing coming over here, and why is she looking at me like that?

"Hi, guys," she sings out, giving the rest of the group an absent wave as she circles directly to me—pressing in close, then closer still, so her arm is looped over my shoulders. "Jack, *sweetie*, didn't see you at first." She motions toward the tool. "Remember me telling you about Clarence from work?" She lets out this strained giggle that's as unsettling as having her touch me like this. I'm a hairsbreadth from calling her brother to come take her back to whatever mental ward she's escaped from when she gives me a pointed look that's part pleading and part disdain, and adds, "He was starting to think *I'd made you up!*"

Made me up?

Well, well, well. Looks like Laurel's gotten herself into a bind. And while it couldn't happen to a more deserving, pricklier wet blanket, I'd be a pretty shitty friend to her brother if I left her hanging. So I do what anyone in my situation would.

Wrapping my arm around her waist, I cinch her in tight and, giving her a look I can only hope has one-tenth the sap in it of Hank and Abby's shared looks, I grin.

"Babe, why didn't you tell me I was finally gonna meet him?" Sticking out my hand to shake and then waiting for him to notice, since he seems well and truly mesmerized by the rest of the table, I add, "Pull up a chair, man. Join us."

Laurel's breath catches and her head snaps around, pure murder in her eyes.

Oh, hell yes, this is going to be fun.

---

Thank you for reading DIRTY PLAYER! **CLICK HERE FOR A SEXY FUN BONUS SCENE WITH GREG & JULIA!**

Can't wait to get your hands on Jack? Snag your copy here **DIRTY BAD BOY**!

Can't wait for more Slayer's Hockey? Skip ahead for Greg's little sister Natalie and his oldest rival Vaughn in **DIRTY SECRET** - Available Now!

---

One-click **DIRTY BAD BOY**! now!

Want to stay in the know about all my new releases? Sign up for my **newsletter** and follow me on **BookBub**.

Also, you're invited to join the party! **Click here to get in on all the fun with my reader group, Mira Lyn Kelly's Book Bunnies**—we'd love to have you :-)

And lastly, I can't tell you how much I appreciate your help in spreading the word about DIRTY PLAYER, including telling a friend. Reviews help readers find books!

Please consider **leaving a review** on your favorite book site. Every one makes a huge difference!

((HUGS))

*Mira*

Also by Mira Lyn Kelly

**SLAYERS HOCKEY**

DIRTY SECRET (Vaughn & Natalie)

DIRTY HOOKUP (Quinn & George)

DIRTY REBOUND (Rux & Cammy)

DIRTY TALKER (Wade & Harlow)

DIRTY DEAL (Axel & Nora)

DIRTY CHRISTMAS (Noel & Misty)

DIRTY GROOM (Diesel & Stormy)

DIRTY D-MAN (Bowie & Piper)

DIRTY DARE (Gulls & Cam)

DIRTY FLIRT (Boomer & Lara)

**BACK TO YOU**

HARD CRUSH (Hank & Abby)

DIRTY PLAYER (Greg & Julia)

DIRTY BAD BOY (Jack & Laurel)

**THE DARE TO LOVE NOVELS**

TRUTH OR DARE (Tyler & Maggie)

TOUCH & GO (Sam & Ava)

NOW & THEN (Ford & Brynn)

**THE WEDDING DATE BOOKS**

MAY THE BEST MAN WIN (Jase & Emily)

THE WEDDING DATE BARGAIN (Max & Sara)

JUST THIS ONCE (Sean & Molly)

DECOY DATE (Brody & Gwen)

**COMING AROUND AGAIN (Re-releases from my early Mira Lyn Kelly & Moira McTark days)**

Just Friends (Matt & Nikki)

All In (Lanie & Jason)

Front Page Affair (Nate & Payton)

The S Before Ex (Ryan & Claire)

Waking Up Married (Connor & Megan)

Once is Never Enough (Garrett & Nichole)

# Acknowledgments

With every book I put out, I become more and more convinced that writing is a team sport. While I'm the one putting the words on the page, there is an amazing group of people cheering, encouraging, supporting, hand holding, inspiring, listening, commiserating, offering advice, answering weird questions, and occasionally rescuing me along the way. I could not do this without them.

I'd like to thank Lexi Ryan, Annika Martin, Zoe York, Jessica Alcazar, Adriana Anders, Kait Nolan, Lisa Kuhne, Shari Slade, Skye Warren, Holly Mortimer, Helene Cuji, Jennifer Haymore, Samantha Potter, Give Me Books Productions, Nicole Resciniti, all the girls from Slack, the awesome PJ Party girls, my review team and eagle eye readers, the family of parents and coaches from the 12U and Peewee hockey teams, and most of all, my wonderful family.

And I'd like to thank you, the reader, for picking up the stories I love write when there are so many out there to choose from. Thank you for your emails, your reviews, and your heartfelt enthusiasm when you're telling a friend about the book you just devoured.

Thank you—I love you guys!!

((hugs))
Mira

## About the Author

Hard core romantic, stress baker, and housekeeper non-extraordinaire, Mira Lyn Kelly is the USA TODAY bestselling author of more than two dozen sizzly love stories with over a million readers worldwide. Growing up in the Chicago area, she earned her degree in Fine Arts from Loyola University and met the love of her life while studying abroad in Rome, Italy… only to discover he'd been living right around the corner from her back home. Having spent her twenties working and playing in the Windy City, she's now settled with her family of eight (including two ridiculous dogs) in beautiful Minnesota. www.miralynkelly.com

Looking to stay in touch and keep up with my new releases, sales and giveaways?? Join my newsletter at miralynkelly.com/newsletter and my Facebook reader group at MiraLynKellybookbunnies. We'd love to have you!!

Printed in Great Britain
by Amazon

40489003R00146